5-G Challenge

Doing Life with God in the Picture

Small Group Leader's Guidebook

WILLOW CREEK RESOURCES®

Life Application Activities, Discussion Questions, Community Building Ideas

Small Group Leader's Guidebook
5-G Challenge: Doing Life with God in the Picture
Winter Quarter Grades 2/3

ISBN 0-744-125-383

Requests for information should be addressed to:
Willow Creek Association
P.O. Box 3188
Barrington, IL 60011-3188

Executive Director of Promiseland: Sue Miller

Executive Director of Promiseland Publishing: Nancy Raney

Creative Team: Deanna Armentrout, Deb Callear, Pat Cimo, David Huber, Kevin Koesterer, Holly Laurent, Dan Lueders, Sue Miller, Susan Shadid, Mindy Stoms, Tom Swartz, Jill Tweeten, Christy Weygandt

Editorial Team: Jorie Dahlin, Janet Quinn, Nancy Raney

Designer: Kathee Biaggne
Cover and Interior Illustrator: Peter Whitehead

Many thanks to: the Promiseland staff team as a whole who continually contributes, our volunteers who help put supplies together each weekend, and the volunteers who try out, test, and evaluate this curriculum to give us feedback along the way.

Printed in the United States of America.

Small Group Leader's Guidebook Table of Contents

5-G Challenge Winter Quarter

Introduction
to Small Groups

Why Have Small Groups?

Group is one of the 5-Gs. We want kids to experience **friendships in community** where they can know and be known, love and be loved, and celebrate and be celebrated.

Developing a 5-G children's ministry means creating a ministry in which relationships can be built. Life change happens best within the context of relationships, and Small Groups can serve as the structure for relationships to develop and grow.

Who Leads a Small Group?

The ministry model for the Promiseland Curriculum includes a structured Small Group Time. This time, during which the same eight to ten kids and one Shepherd-Leader meet together weekly, is the key time for relationships and community to be built and for children to begin to see the relevant application of the Bible truth to everyday life. Because the main goal of Small Groups is to build relationships and intentionally shepherd the children, the leader of the Small Group is someone who has the spiritual gift of shepherding and is called a Small Group Leader. Below is a chart showing the difference between a Small Group Leader and a Teacher.

The following characteristics have been identified as those of effective children's Small Group Leaders:

1. They see their role as facilitators to apply the curriculum. They take what was taught in Large Group and put it into action.
2. They create an environment in which relationships can develop:
   - They make sure the environment is physically, emotionally, and spiritually safe.
   - They speak to the children in respectful ways.
   - They ask the children questions.

Teacher	Small Group Leader
Curriculum is taught	Curriculum is applied
Children learn something	Children relate to the leader
Children associate the teacher as being with the children's ministy	Children associate the leader as being a part of their lives, both in and outside of children's ministry
	Lifetime friendships can be developed
	Hearts are touched
	Children feel cared for
	Children long for more

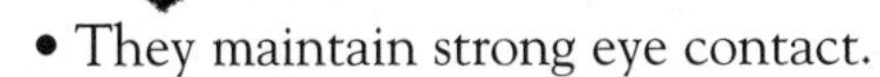

- They maintain strong eye contact.
- They listen carefully.
- They use appropriate touch.
- They are on time to greet the children.
- They arrive prepared.
- They relate well with the children.

3 They want to know the children and want children to know each other.

4 They provide focused attention with the children during Activity Stations, Kid Connection, Small Group Time, and time outside of the ministry (within stated guidelines.)

5 They have a desire to help children develop spiritually and become more Christ-like.

- They share their own personal spiritual development.
- They pray for the children.
- They model Christ-likeness.

6 They encourage children verbally, with body language, and with written notes or cards.

7 They connect with the children's parents.

- They introduce themselves to the parents.
- They inquire about the rest of the family.
- They inform parents about their child's participation in the ministry.
- They invite parents to be a part of the ministry.

How Do Small Groups Fit Into the Lesson?

There are two times during the lesson in which Small Groups meet together. The first time is just prior to the Large Group Program. As children enter the room in which the Large Group Program will take place, they find their Small Group Leaders and sit with their Small Groups. They then participate in Kid Connection.

Kid Connection is a five-minute time for the group members to connect. Questions are asked to encourage the children to share on a personal level. For example, "What is your idea of a perfect Saturday?" "If you could spend fifteen minutes with any one person, who would it be?" Often the question is loosely tied to the Key Concept of the lesson. After the children have answered the question, the Small Group Leader lets the group know a little bit about what will happen in the Large Group Program and what to look for in the story.

The second time Small Groups meet together is after the Large Group Program. This is called Small Group Time and is usually twenty minutes in length. This is the key time for intentional shepherding to occur and is designed to build community. The Small Group Leaders aid in the application of the teaching as well as minister to the kids personally. It is in the Small Group Time that each child becomes well known and receives encouragement. They are given an example of authentic Christianity as the leader shares his or her life with them. Children are helped to grow in their faith. During this time, children participate in fun learning activities that make the Bible lessons relevant to their lives. Usually, the lesson's NOW WHAT? Objective is addressed during the Small Group Time. Through application-oriented games, conversation, and prayer with their Small Group Leaders, kids explore ways to live out the biblical truths taught during the Large Group Program.

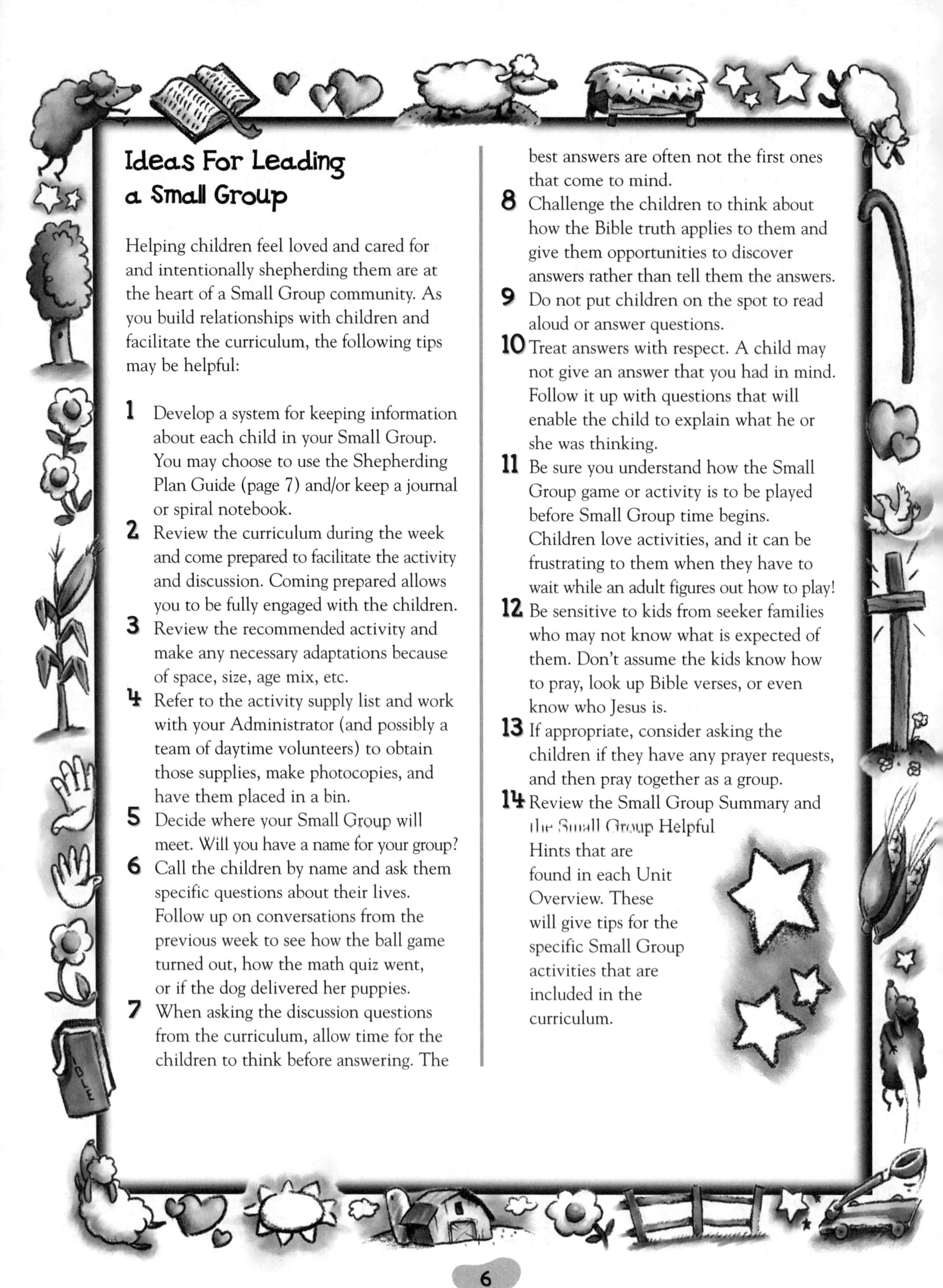

Ideas For Leading a Small Group

Helping children feel loved and cared for and intentionally shepherding them are at the heart of a Small Group community. As you build relationships with children and facilitate the curriculum, the following tips may be helpful:

1. Develop a system for keeping information about each child in your Small Group. You may choose to use the Shepherding Plan Guide (page 7) and/or keep a journal or spiral notebook.
2. Review the curriculum during the week and come prepared to facilitate the activity and discussion. Coming prepared allows you to be fully engaged with the children.
3. Review the recommended activity and make any necessary adaptations because of space, size, age mix, etc.
4. Refer to the activity supply list and work with your Administrator (and possibly a team of daytime volunteers) to obtain those supplies, make photocopies, and have them placed in a bin.
5. Decide where your Small Group will meet. Will you have a name for your group?
6. Call the children by name and ask them specific questions about their lives. Follow up on conversations from the previous week to see how the ball game turned out, how the math quiz went, or if the dog delivered her puppies.
7. When asking the discussion questions from the curriculum, allow time for the children to think before answering. The best answers are often not the first ones that come to mind.
8. Challenge the children to think about how the Bible truth applies to them and give them opportunities to discover answers rather than tell them the answers.
9. Do not put children on the spot to read aloud or answer questions.
10. Treat answers with respect. A child may not give an answer that you had in mind. Follow it up with questions that will enable the child to explain what he or she was thinking.
11. Be sure you understand how the Small Group game or activity is to be played before Small Group time begins. Children love activities, and it can be frustrating to them when they have to wait while an adult figures out how to play!
12. Be sensitive to kids from seeker families who may not know what is expected of them. Don't assume the kids know how to pray, look up Bible verses, or even know who Jesus is.
13. If appropriate, consider asking the children if they have any prayer requests, and then pray together as a group.
14. Review the Small Group Summary and the Small Group Helpful Hints that are found in each Unit Overview. These will give tips for the specific Small Group activities that are included in the curriculum.

Shepherding Plan Guide

How Well Am I Building the Relationship?

Children are fearfully and wonderfully made. Each one is unique and special, and designed and loved by God. Often times, the children do not know this truth. The chart below is a simple tool that can help Leaders know their children and help the children understand they are God's wonderful creations. This chart is meant to help you, as a Small Group Leader, shepherd your Small Group.

Key Areas/What do I know?	Names of Group Members: 1	2	3	4	5	6	7	8	9	10
Family History										
Family Information?										
Spiritual Information?										
Key Questions: Do I know . . .										
How this child expresses love and how he or she needs love expressed to him or her?										
How this child learns best?										
What makes this child sad?										
What makes this child happy?										
What frightens this child?										
What this child likes to do?										
Who this child's heroes are? Why he or she chose them as heroes?										
Which people or characters are influential in the life of this child?										
What key interests this child has?										
Church History										
How long has this child been in this children's ministry?										
What are this child's church experiences?										
What is this child's favorite thing about coming to this children's ministry program?										
Has this child told his or her friends about this children's ministry?										

PRAYING FOR THE CHILDREN YOU SHEPHERD

The Bible has many examples of Jesus talking about children. Here are a few for you to use as inspirations for your prayers.

Matthew 18:3

And He said: "I tell you the truth, unless you change and become like little children, you will never enter the kingdom of heaven."

My Prayer:

Matthew 19:14

Jesus said, "Let the little children come to Me, and do not hinder them, for the kingdom of heaven belongs to such as these."

My Prayer:

Mark 9:37

"Whoever welcomes one of these little children in My name welcomes Me; and whoever welcomes Me does not welcome Me but the One who sent Me."

My Prayer:

Unit 1 Overview
God's Unstoppable Love

Unit Summary

This first unit of the Winter Quarter helps children learn and understand the Christmas story. Kids will learn that God loves us so much that He sent His Son to earth as a baby. His love could not be stopped by any person or circumstance—it was "unstoppable." In Lesson 1, they will see a creative narrative showing how many times the Christmas story might have been different based on people's choices. Next, they will have an opportunity to celebrate Christmas in an extended Small Group and music time. Through a video in Lesson 3, they will learn that God wouldn't allow anything to stop His wonderful plan to redeem the world. Lesson 4 contains a video entitled, "The Littlest Shepherd." From this, children will learn they are never too big or too little for Christmas. Finally, through the story of Anna and Simeon, kids will learn to thank God and remember all He has done for them.

Lesson Overviews

Lesson 1

God's Unstoppable Plan
Luke 1:26-32; 2:1-16; Matthew 1:22, 23
Key Concept: God shows His unstoppable love by giving us His Son, Jesus.
Bible Verse: "But the angel said to them, 'Do not be afraid. I bring you good news of great joy that will be for all the people.' " Luke 2:10
Know What (LG): Children will hear that Jesus was born a baby in Bethlehem. They will hear that God's love is unstoppable.
So What (LG): Children will learn that God loves us so much that He sent His Son, Jesus. He left heaven and came down to earth in the form of a baby.
Now What (SG): Children will create psalms, poems, drawings, songs, and raps to show their thanks for God's gift, Jesus.
Spiritual Formation:
Celebration/Thanksgiving
5-G: Grace/Group

Lesson 2

Small Group Celebration
Luke 2:1-16
Key Concept: God wants us to come together to celebrate the birth of Jesus.
Bible Verse: "Glory to God in the highest." Luke 2:14
Know What (LG): Children will sing and participate in a Large Group music time to celebrate Jesus' birth.
So What (SG): Children will celebrate and reflect with their Small Group what they have learned about Grace, Growth, Group, Gifts, and Good Stewardship.
Now What (SG): Children will participate in an extended Small Group time with their leader and celebrate community with one another. They will hear specific affirmations from their Small Group Leader and reflect upon the birth of Jesus.
Spiritual Formation:
Celebration/Community
5-G: Growth/Group

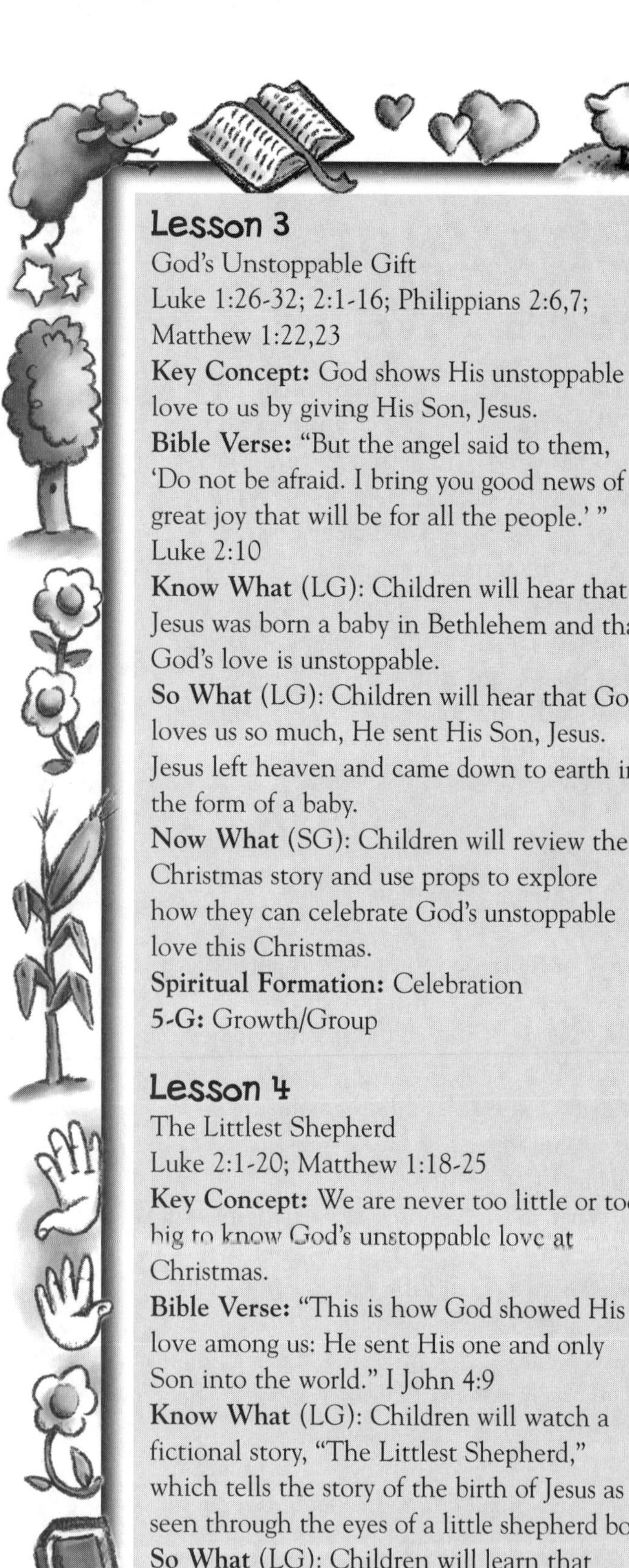

Lesson 3

God's Unstoppable Gift
Luke 1:26-32; 2:1-16; Philippians 2:6,7; Matthew 1:22,23
Key Concept: God shows His unstoppable love to us by giving His Son, Jesus.
Bible Verse: "But the angel said to them, 'Do not be afraid. I bring you good news of great joy that will be for all the people.' " Luke 2:10
Know What (LG): Children will hear that Jesus was born a baby in Bethlehem and that God's love is unstoppable.
So What (LG): Children will hear that God loves us so much, He sent His Son, Jesus. Jesus left heaven and came down to earth in the form of a baby.
Now What (SG): Children will review the Christmas story and use props to explore how they can celebrate God's unstoppable love this Christmas.
Spiritual Formation: Celebration
5-G: Growth/Group

Lesson 4

The Littlest Shepherd
Luke 2:1-20; Matthew 1:18-25
Key Concept: We are never too little or too big to know God's unstoppable love at Christmas.
Bible Verse: "This is how God showed His love among us: He sent His one and only Son into the world." I John 4:9
Know What (LG): Children will watch a fictional story, "The Littlest Shepherd," which tells the story of the birth of Jesus as seen through the eyes of a little shepherd boy.
So What (LG): Children will learn that God, through His love, sent Jesus into the world and He wants everyone, young and old, to know Jesus.
Now What (SG): Children will participate in an activity to discover ways they can get to know Jesus.
Spiritual Formation: Friendship/Knowledge
5-G: Growth/Group

Lesson 5

Anna and Simeon
Luke 2:21-40
Key Concept: We can thank God because His unstoppable love is for all time.
Bible Verse: "Remember the wonders He has done." Psalm 105:5
Know What (LG): Children will hear the story of Anna and Simeon at the temple with baby Jesus.
So What (LG): Children will learn that God is good, and we can thank Him for what He has done.
Now What (SG): Children will participate in an activity to remember some of the good things God has done for them this past year and thank Him.
Spiritual Formation: Thankfulness/Trust
5-G: Growth/Group

Large Group Presentation Summary

Each Large Group Program in this unit celebrates God's unstoppable love that He expressed to us through the birth of Jesus at Christmas. Lesson 1 is a detective-style drama of the Christmas story. Lesson 2 is a Small Group celebration, so no Large Group Program is presented. Lesson 3 is presented on video, teaching kids that nothing could stop God's unstoppable love. Lesson 4 utilizes a video drama entitled, "The Littlest Shepherd" to show kids they are never too little or too big for the Christmas story.

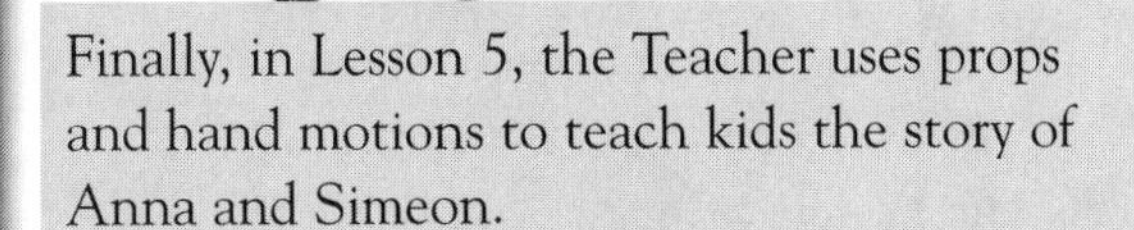

Finally, in Lesson 5, the Teacher uses props and hand motions to teach kids the story of Anna and Simeon.

Large Group Helpful Hints

1. Lesson 1 is identical for Grades 2/3 and 4/5, so you can combine the two for the Large Group Program.
2. In the drama in Lesson 1, three kids from the audience will be asked to volunteer to help in the drama. Pick these kids at the beginning of the Pre-Teach, so the other actors have time to tell them what to expect, where they will be taken when they enter, and to move when they are directed by the actors.
3. You may combine the age levels of Kindergarten – Grade 5 for the music celebration in Lesson 2 if you'd like.
4. Here are a few tips if you choose to do Lesson 3 live instead of showing the video: Record a booming voice to use as God talking to Gabriel during the lesson. As you move from station to station, try not to stand with your back to the kids—in order to keep them engaged, you will need to be facing them and acting with great enthusiasm. If you don't have carpet blocks or small platforms for each station, you might want to put yellow tape on the floor around each station, and tell the kids to sit outside the yellow tape. Also, be sure there is a clear path from station to station for the Teacher and Assistant.
5. For Lessons 3 and 4, you can combine Grades K-5 for the Large Group Program.
6. In Lesson 5, the story of Anna and Simeon in the temple is told by pulling out key words and putting them up like a Scrabble® gameboard. When all of the words are up, it will spell "thank you." The kids will learn a key phrase for each portion of the story, and the teacher has the option of using props or hand motions for each phrase. The goal is that by the end of the story, the children will be able to repeat back each phrase and tell the story back to the Teacher. Decide whether you will use props or hand motions and have fun with it!
7. If you do not have enough Small Group Leaders because of the Christmas holidays, turn the Small Group lessons into Teacher-led Large Group Activities. For example, in Lesson 4, instead of using marshmallows and toothpicks, pick kids to come up to the front of the room, answer a question, and then build a building out of tinker toys.

Small Group Summary

This Christmas unit gives Small Group Leaders the opportunity to celebrate Christmas and build community within their Small Groups. Lesson 1 gives kids the chance to create their own psalms, poems, drawings, and songs to God. Lesson 2 is a Small Group Celebration, where groups will complete a short activity and then celebrate however they choose. In Lesson 3, kids will look at the Christmas story, and how their families celebrate the holiday. A building game is used in Lesson 4 to help kids learn how to "build" their relationships with God. Finally, in Lesson 5, kids will have fun while playing a drawing game and thinking about things for which they are thankful.

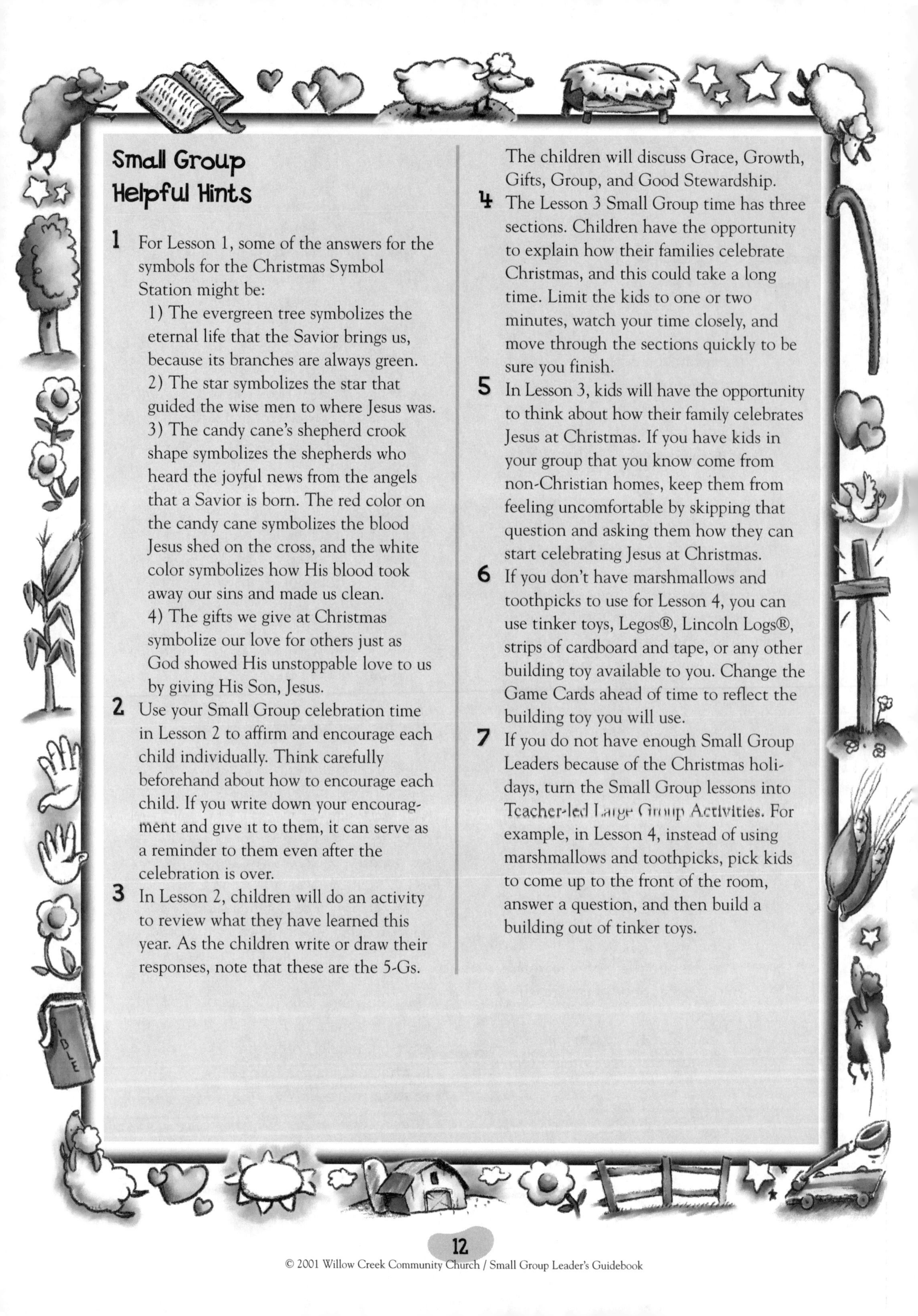

Small Group Helpful Hints

1 For Lesson 1, some of the answers for the symbols for the Christmas Symbol Station might be:

1) The evergreen tree symbolizes the eternal life that the Savior brings us, because its branches are always green.

2) The star symbolizes the star that guided the wise men to where Jesus was.

3) The candy cane's shepherd crook shape symbolizes the shepherds who heard the joyful news from the angels that a Savior is born. The red color on the candy cane symbolizes the blood Jesus shed on the cross, and the white color symbolizes how His blood took away our sins and made us clean.

4) The gifts we give at Christmas symbolize our love for others just as God showed His unstoppable love to us by giving His Son, Jesus.

2 Use your Small Group celebration time in Lesson 2 to affirm and encourage each child individually. Think carefully beforehand about how to encourage each child. If you write down your encouragment and give it to them, it can serve as a reminder to them even after the celebration is over.

3 In Lesson 2, children will do an activity to review what they have learned this year. As the children write or draw their responses, note that these are the 5-Gs. The children will discuss Grace, Growth, Gifts, Group, and Good Stewardship.

4 The Lesson 3 Small Group time has three sections. Children have the opportunity to explain how their families celebrate Christmas, and this could take a long time. Limit the kids to one or two minutes, watch your time closely, and move through the sections quickly to be sure you finish.

5 In Lesson 3, kids will have the opportunity to think about how their family celebrates Jesus at Christmas. If you have kids in your group that you know come from non-Christian homes, keep them from feeling uncomfortable by skipping that question and asking them how they can start celebrating Jesus at Christmas.

6 If you don't have marshmallows and toothpicks to use for Lesson 4, you can use tinker toys, Legos®, Lincoln Logs®, strips of cardboard and tape, or any other building toy available to you. Change the Game Cards ahead of time to reflect the building toy you will use.

7 If you do not have enough Small Group Leaders because of the Christmas holidays, turn the Small Group lessons into Teacher-led Large Group Activities. For example, in Lesson 4, instead of using marshmallows and toothpicks, pick kids to come up to the front of the room, answer a question, and then build a building out of tinker toys.

Unit 1: God's Unstoppable Love

God's Unstoppable Plan

Challenge the children in your ministry this Winter Quarter as you present four of the 5-Gs: **Grace**, **Growth**, **Group**, and **Gift**. Unit 1 powerfully illustrates the **Group** and **Grace** "Gs" as Small Groups celebrate Christmas and kids hear about the "Unstoppable Love" God showed when He sent His Son, Jesus, to earth. In Unit 2, **Growth** and **Gift** are emphasized as kids learn from Jesus' example how to live "The Extreme Life." This quarter ends with Unit 3, "Show Me the Shepherd." Children will **Grow** as they explore how we are like sheep and Jesus is our Good Shepherd, and experience **Grace** when they hear the salvation message. Throughout the quarter, kids will learn more about what it means to "do life with God in the picture."

BIBLE SUMMARY

Luke 1:26-32; 2:1-16; Matthew 1:22, 23

The Bible says that God provided an unstoppable plan by sending His Son, Jesus, as a baby to be born of a virgin named Mary. Jesus, named Immanuel, means "God with us." Through the events of the Christmas story, we see that nothing was going to stop God's plan to send Jesus. God's incredible love for us is UNSTOPPABLE!

KEY CONCEPT
God shows His unstoppable love by giving us His Son, Jesus.

BIBLE VERSE

"But the angel said to them, 'Do not be afraid. I bring you good news of great joy that will be for all the people.' " Luke 2:10

OBJECTIVES

KNOW WHAT (LG): Children will hear that Jesus was born a baby in Bethlehem. They will hear that God's love is unstoppable.

SO WHAT (LG): Children will learn that God loves us so much that He sent His Son, Jesus. He left heaven and came down to earth in the form of a baby.

NOW WHAT (SG): Children will create psalms, poems, drawings, songs, and raps to show their thanks for God's gift, Jesus.

SPIRITUAL FORMATION

Celebration/Thanksgiving

5-G

Grace/Group

IN ADVANCE
(DONE BY YOUR ADMINISTRATOR)

- Photocopy and cut out Bible Verse Cards—one per child (page 25 in *Administrator's Guidebook*).
- Photocopy Station Cards—one of each per group (pages 18-24 in *Administrator's Guidebook*).
- Gather pencils—one per child.
- Gather sets of colored pencils—one set per group.
- Gather sheets of colored paper—thirty-five sheets per group.
- Place the above-mentioned items in a bin for each Small Group Leader.

LEADER'S PREP

Read Luke 1:26-32; 2:1-16; and Matthew 1:22, 23. Around Christmas, many Americans watch a TV special called, *How The Grinch Stole Christmas*. The Grinch is a miserable character who hates Christmas and decides to put a stop to it by stealing all the presents, bells, trees, and holiday food. He thinks by taking away all the trimmings of Christmas, he will stop Christmas. Some of us can really identify with the Grinch. Deep down, we may not want to wrap another present, sign another card, put up one more decoration, hear one more carol, or eat one more candy cane. Even the best of us find it hard not to be like Grinch sometimes. To avoid becoming like Grinch, reflect on what it might be like to awaken on Christmas morning to find the usual trimmings replaced: no trees, except the tree Jesus died on; no star, except the star that pointed wise men to Him; no gifts, except the gift of eternal and abundant life; no lights, except the light of God's unchanging Word; no Christmas feasts, except the bread of life which when eaten, one will live forever; and no Christmas parades, except for the parade of joy, peace, and thanksgiving that continues to pour out of you because of His unstoppable love.

KID CONNECTION

(5 minutes)

WELCOME the kids to your Small Group.
ASK how their week went.
CONTINUE, "What kind of holiday traditions does your family do at Christmas? Why do you do these traditions at Christmas?"
SHARE about your holiday traditions and why you do them.

TRANSITION

SAY, "There is usually a true and wonderful story behind all of our traditions. The Christmas tradition that Christians celebrate is no different. The story behind God's plan to send Jesus as the Savior of the world is wonderful, but many of us don't think about how impossible the story is without God's power. That's right! Without God's power, Christmas might have looked completely different to us. Do you want to know how different Christmas might have looked if God hadn't showed up? Watch to see what happens in Large Group."

SMALL GROUP

(20 minutes)

REVIEW

SAY, "Which Bible character do you think needed God's help the most and why?"
EXPLAIN, "Today we want to spend some time thinking about just how impossible it would have been for the Christmas story to happen without God's power and unstoppable love."

ACTIVITY: PRAISE AND THANK YOU STATIONS

The purpose of this activity is to give kids an opportunity to express their thanks for all God has done for them through seven different ways of expression.

SUPPLIES PROVIDED BY YOUR ADMINISTRATOR

- ❍ Station Cards
- ❍ Pencils
- ❍ Colored pencils
- ❍ Colored paper (5 per station)

SET-UP

PLACE the seven Station Cards on the floor or on the wall within the area where your Small Group meets.
PLACE pencils and colored paper at each station.
SET the colored pencils at the Christmas Thank You Art Station.

INSTRUCTIONS

SAY, "Today we are going to talk about just how unstoppable God's love is. It says in the Bible, "The angel said to them, 'Do not be afraid. I bring you good news of great joy that will be for all the people' " Luke 2:10. This good news is Jesus. God's love is unstoppable and we saw how the Christmas story we celebrate each year began with God's power. One thing we can do to tell God we love Him is to spend some time giving God thanks and praise for His amazing gift to us."

CONTINUE, "There are seven Praise and Thank You Stations around us today. Each station has directions for you to read and follow. We can work as a group, in teams of two or three, or individually at these stations and give God a special kind of thank you!"

BEGIN the activity.
GATHER kids back into the circle after 10 minutes.
SAY, "Let's share all of these thank you notes, poems, pictures, psalms, and raps with each other to thank God for His unstoppable love."
HAVE children share what is on their papers.

SHEPHERDING TIP

Encourage kids to remember that these expressions of thanks and praise to God are prayers of thanksgiving and praise for God's unstoppable love; therefore, a quiet atmosphere is helpful, except for at the Rap/Poem Staiton.

WRAP-UP

SAY, "God is pleased when we share these expressions of thanks and praise with each other and with Him. They are ways of telling God thanks for showing love that is unstoppable. That means nothing can stop God's love from coming. **GOD SHOWS HIS UNSTOPPABLE LOVE BY GIVING US HIS SON, JESUS.**"

BIBLE VERSE

GIVE a Bible Verse Card to each child and repeat the verse together. "But the angel said to them, 'Do not be afraid. I bring you good news of great joy that will be for all the people.' " Luke 2:10
REMIND the kids, "This verse reminds us that God gave us His Son, Jesus, born to save us."

PRAYER

Dear God,

Thank You for all You did to make Christmas possible. Today we rapped for You, drew for You, and read poems and thank you notes to You. We did all this because You showed Your unstoppable love to us that very first Christmas. Amen.

KID CONNECTION CONTINUES . . .

Small Group Leaders, use this time to continue to build community and learn more about your kids and their concerns. Listen closely so you are better equipped to pray for and reach out to each child.

ASK, "What gift can you give to Jesus on His birthday?"

Unit 1: God's Unstoppable Love

Small Group Celebration

Challenge the children in your ministry this Winter Quarter as you present four of the 5-Gs: **Grace**, **Growth**, **Group**, and **Gift**. Unit 1 powerfully illustrates the **Group** and **Grace** "Gs" as Small Groups celebrate Christmas and kids hear about the "Unstoppable Love" God showed when He sent His Son, Jesus, to earth. In Unit 2, **Growth** and **Gift** are emphasized as kids learn from Jesus' example how to live "The Extreme Life." This quarter ends with Unit 3, "Show Me the Shepherd." Children will **Grow** as they explore how we are like sheep and Jesus is our Good Shepherd, and experience **Grace** when they hear the salvation message. Throughout the quarter, kids will learn more about what it means to "do life with God in the picture."

BIBLE SUMMARY

Luke 2:1-16

The Bible tells the magnificent story of Jesus' birth. Not only has God given us the gift of His Son, Jesus, but He has also given us one another. Today we will celebrate His birth with a time of praise and worship by singing Christmas music in Large Group. Then, in Small Group, we have intentionally set aside time for Small Groups to review what they have learned over the past few months and celebrate the birth of Christ. During the forty minutes of celebrating Small Group life together, children will hear specific affirmations from their Small Group Leader and celebrate God's gift to us.

KEY CONCEPT
God wants us to come together to celebrate the birth of Jesus.

BIBLE VERSE

"Glory to God in the highest." Luke 2:14

OBJECTIVES

KNOW WHAT: (LG) Children will sing and participate in a Large Group music time to celebrate Jesus' birth.
SO WHAT: (SG) Children will celebrate and reflect with their Small Group what they have learned about Grace, Growth, Group, Gifts, and Good Stewardship.
NOW WHAT: (SG) Children will participate in an extended Small Group Time with their leader and celebrate community with one another. They will hear specific affirmations from their Small Group Leader and reflect upon the birth of Jesus.

SPIRITUAL FORMATION

Celebration/Community

5-G

Growth/Group

IN ADVANCE
(DONE BY YOUR ADMINISTRATOR)

- Photocopy and cut out Bible Verse Cards—one per child (page 27 in *Administrator's Guidebook*).
- Gather markers—one per child.
- Photocopy the Christmas Star—one per child (page 26 in *Administrator's Guidebook*).
- Place the above-mentioned items in a bin for each Small Group Leader.

LEADER'S PREP

Read Luke 2:1-16. Christmas brings people together. Families join together to celebrate this wondrous event. People attend parties, gather to sing, play, and enjoy each other's company. What a great time of year! You have the opportunity during Small Group Time to celebrate the birth of Jesus with your group. What an awesome time to get to know your kids better as you do a fun activity or just talk. Take advantage of this wonderful time. You know your group of kids and what they will like, so plan accordingly. Take some time this week to reflect and pray for each of the kids in your group. What ways can you encourage them? What are their strengths, and what do they bring to your Small Group? Make sure you come prepared to celebrate each of them in a special way. This may be the most meaningful Christmas present they receive this year.

LEADER'S NOTE

The following activity will help you review what the kids have learned this year. If you did not use the 5-G *Challenge* Fall Quarter curriculum, you can change the phrases to future tense. For example, "We will learn that God loves us very much." Or, you might want to skip this activity altogether and use the time for your Christmas celebration.

SMALL GROUP
(40 minutes)

WELCOME the kids to your Small Group.

SAY, "That was a fun music celebration. Singing songs to God gives us an opportunity to tell Him thanks and celebrate all He does for us, especially for the birth of Jesus. Our Bible verse for today says, 'Glory to God in the highest.' When we sing, we give God glory, which means we give Him all the credit for what He's given us."

GIVE a star and marker to each child.

HAVE each child write his or her name on the back of the star.

SAY, "We are going to do some fun activities today. To start our celebration, I'd like to take some time to see what we have learned this year about God and how we have grown in our friendship with Him. On this star we will write or draw the things that we have learned and what we are thankful for this year. On the middle of the star it says, 'God's unstoppable love can shine through me.' This activity will help us see five ways God shows His unstoppable love to us and how we can show that love to others."

CONTINUE, "Let's start with the first one. We have learned that God loves us very much and wants to be our friend. He wants all people to be His forever friend. Think about one person you know who doesn't know God and whom you could tell about God. Maybe it is a friend or a family member."

HAVE each child draw or write the name on the point of the star that has the number one.

SAY, "We also learned that God wants us to grow in our friendship with Him. We can do that by reading the Bible, praying, and obeying what He tells us in the Bible."

HAVE children write or draw one way they got to know God better on the number two point of their star.

SAY, "We have also talked about how God wants us to use our talents to serve Him and others. A few examples include serving at a homeless shelter, volunteering at church, or helping a neighbor, family, or friends."

HAVE children write down one way they served God or others on the number three point of their star.

SAY, "Finally, we learned how we can be

people that give our time and money to others. God tells us that as His friends, He wants us to be giving people. A few examples include giving food to those in need, presents to needy kids, or money to those who have little."

HAVE children write or draw one way they have given to others on the number four point of their star.

SAY, "The last thing we have learned so far this year is that God gives us people in our lives with whom we can get to know and who can get to know us. These friends are special because they help us out when we need it and cheer us on when we have done something great. This is a place where we can learn more about God together, and we can have friendships with others who want to help us grow in our friendship with God."

HAVE children write down one thing they like about their group on the number five point of their star.

SHEPHERDING TIP
If you have seeker kids in your Small Group, have them write down one thing they like about coming here this year.

SAY, "These five things are wonderful ways God helps us grow. Take these stars home with you and hang them where you can be reminded that God has unstoppable love for you, and He wants to spread that love through you to others in these five ways. We've had so much fun getting to know each other this year. I'd like to spend some time telling you about what you each bring to our group."

ACTIVITY: CHRISTMAS CELEBRATION

The purpose of today's Small Group is to individually affirm each child in your group. This will be a very meaningful time for your group. If you've made something special for your kids, you can share it with them. You can choose from the list of activities that are provided or you can be as individually creative as you'd like. You may bring treats, crafts, games, or any other surprises to celebrate with your group.

CELEBRATION IDEAS:

1. Have a birthday party for Jesus. Bring in party hats, favors, a birthday cake, or cupcakes. Let the children share what they would like to give to Jesus as a birthday gift. Don't forget to sing "Happy Birthday" to Jesus.
2. Bring in materials for the kids to make Christmas ornaments or bookmarks for their friends and family.
3. Give each child a small gift (i.e. candy bar or candy cane.) As you present the gift to each child, tell him or her why you like having him or her in your group. Wish each child a Merry Christmas.
4. Bring in colored paper, markers, or small craft items and let the kids make cards for each other or their friends and family. Encourage them to write a personal note to their friends in their Small Group.
5. Bring in a small snack and have a fun time sharing together.
6. Bring in colored paper, stickers, baseball cards, etc. Have each child in your group write their name and decorate a colored piece of paper. Allow all the kids in the group to go around and sign each other's papers, writing each other encouraging notes.
7. Bring in board games for your group to play.
8. Bring in a Polaroid camera, a posterboard, and decorations. Cut the posterboard into a Christmas tree shape and make a Small Group Christmas tree using the pictures of the kids for ornaments.

9 If you are leading a group of seekers or serving as a substitute, you might use a nativity scene brought from home, or have kids create the characters in the nativity scene. Use the nativity scene to tell or act out the story of Jesus' birth.

WRAP UP

REMEMBER to spend some time affirming each child if you haven't done so already.

BIBLE VERSE

GIVE a Bible Verse Card to each child and repeat the verse together. "Glory to God in the highest." Luke 2:14

REMIND the kids, "This verse reminds us that Christmas is a time to celebrate the unstoppable love God has for us, and to give glory and praise to God."

PRAYER

Dear God,
Thank You for the unstoppable love You expressed to us when You sent Jesus as a baby on Christmas morning. I pray for [*each child in your group by name*]. Help us to celebrate Your gift to us this Christmas. Amen.

Unit 1: God's Unstoppable Love

God's Unstoppable Gift

Challenge the children in your ministry this Winter Quarter as you present four of the 5-Gs: **Grace**, **Growth**, **Group**, and **Gift**. Unit 1 powerfully illustrates the **Group** and **Grace** "Gs" as Small Groups celebrate Christmas and kids hear about the "Unstoppable Love" God showed when He sent His Son, Jesus, to earth. In Unit 2, **Growth** and **Gift** are emphasized as kids learn from Jesus' example how to live "The Extreme Life." This quarter ends with Unit 3, "Show Me the Shepherd." Children will **Grow** as they explore how we are like sheep and Jesus is our Good Shepherd, and experience **Grace** when they hear the salvation message. Throughout the quarter, kids will learn more about what it means to "do life with God in the picture."

BIBLE SUMMARY

Luke 1:26-32; 2:1-16; Philippians 2:6,7; Matthew 1:22,23

The angel Gabriel visited Mary and told her she would give birth to the Son of God. Mary told Joseph, to whom she was engaged. An angel told Joseph in a dream that Mary was telling the truth; she was going to give birth to the Son of God. Mary and Joseph went to Bethlehem for the census. There was no room in the inn, so the couple stayed in a stable, where Mary gave birth to Jesus. The angels gave word of Jesus' birth to the shepherds, who came to see the baby Jesus.

KEY CONCEPT

God shows His unstoppable love to us by giving His Son, Jesus.

BIBLE VERSE

"But the angel said to them, 'Do not be afraid. I bring you good news of great joy that will be for all the people.' " Luke 2:10

OBJECTIVES

KNOW WHAT (LG): Children will hear that Jesus was born a baby in Bethlehem and that God's love is unstoppable.

SO WHAT (LG): Children will hear that God loves us so much, He sent His Son, Jesus. Jesus left heaven and came down to earth in the form of a baby.

NOW WHAT (SG): Children will review the Christmas story and use props to explore how they can celebrate God's unstoppable love this Christmas.

SPIRITUAL FORMATION

Celebration

5-G

Growth/Group

IN ADVANCE

(DONE BY YOUR ADMINISTRATOR)

- Photocopy and cut out Bible Verse Cards—one per child (page 28 in *Administrator's Guidebook*).
- Gather nine different types of small Christmas craft items—each group should have one of each type. You can purchase small craft items from craft stores, each about two inches long, such as: Christmas tree ornament, Christmas stocking, jingle

bell, Christmas tree, Christmas present, toy, or manger. Or you can gather items such as squares of wrapping paper, bits of tinsel, Christmas cards, or Christmas cookies.
- Place the above-mentioned items in a bin for each Small Group Leader.

LEADER'S PREP

Read Luke 1:26-32; 2:1-16; Philippians 2:6,7; Matthew 1:22,23. Sometimes the story of Christmas can seem so familiar. Every year, we see the same Christmas shows and sing the same Christmas songs. But the story of Jesus' birth is far from boring. God sent His Son, Jesus, down to earth as a baby. Jesus' birth was part of God's plan to save us from our sins. That is nothing short of amazing. Do all you can this year to renew your amazement and wonder of this story. Read a new perspective on the story, pray for God to open your heart, and listen to some new Christmas music. Whatever you do, don't miss what God wants to teach you throughout this Christmas season.

KID CONNECTION

(5 minutes)

WELCOME the kids to your Small Group. Take some time to catch up with the children and find out if something special happened this week.

ASK, "If something is 'unstoppable,' what does that mean? Can you think of anything that can be described as unstoppable?"

TRANSITION

SAY, "Two weeks ago, we saw how God's plan was unstoppable. The story of Jesus' birth is the story of God's unstoppable love for us. During Large Group time, listen to hear various times when God's love was unstoppable."

SHEPHERDING TIP

This activity will give you an opportunity to learn more about your kids and their families. Be sure to watch the clock as kids tell their stories, so you have time for the wrap-up questions.

SMALL GROUP

(20 minutes)

REVIEW

ASK, "When in the story was God's love unstoppable?" (*When Joseph didn't want to marry Mary; when there was no room in the inn.*)

SAY, "The story of Jesus' birth is such a wonderful story. **GOD SHOWS HIS UNSTOPPABLE LOVE TO US BY GIVING HIS SON, JESUS**. We celebrate Christmas because of Jesus' birth. Today, we're going to review the Christmas story in our Small Group. We're going to be creative and think about how God's love was unstoppable."

ACTIVITY: CHRISTMAS STORYTELLING

The purpose of this activity is to stretch the children's thinking about Christmas by telling the Christmas story using props.

SUPPLIES PROVIDED BY YOUR ADMINISTRATOR

- ❍ Several small Christmas items

SET UP

SIT in a circle on the floor.
DIVIDE your group into 5 groups—they might be pairs or singles. Assign each person/group to represent one of the following characters from today's story: Angel Gabriel, Mary, Joseph, Innkeeper, Shepherd.

PART 1 INSTRUCTIONS

SAY, "Each of your groups represent one of the characters in today's story. I'm going to give your groups a moment to discuss the following questions, and then you will all share with the group. Your questions are:

1. From your character's view, what happened in today's story?
2. How did your character personally see God's unstoppable love?

GIVE kids a few minutes to discuss in their groups, then go around the circle and have each share their answers.

PART 2 INSTRUCTIONS

PUT the Christmas objects in the center of the circle.
SAY, "Now you have the opportunity to share with the group. In one minute, using at least six of the objects in the center of our circle, explain to the group how your family celebrates Christmas, the birth of Christ."
GO around the circle and have kids briefly share.
ASK the following questions:

1. Think about your family's Christmas celebration. Do you ever think about Jesus' birth as you celebrate? Where does Jesus fit into your celebration?
2. What are some ways you could celebrate Jesus' birth this Christmas? *(display a manger scene, have a birthday cake for Jesus, sing songs about Jesus)*
3. God showed us His unstoppable love by sending Jesus to earth. What are some things you can do to remind people that God loves them this Christmas? *(Tell people about Jesus' birth, give gifts to people we love, donate food or money to people who need it, help our parents prepare for Christmas)*

WRAP UP

SAY, "Today we learned that **GOD SHOWS HIS UNSTOPPABLE LOVE TO US BY GIVING HIS SON, JESUS.** Nothing could stop God from sending Jesus to earth as a baby. What a great gift! As you celebrate Christmas this year, remember the story of God's unstoppable love."

BIBLE VERSE

GIVE a Bible Verse Card to each child and repeat the verse together. "But the angel said to them, 'Do not be afraid. I bring you good news of great joy that will be for all the people.' " Luke 2:10
SAY, "This verse is the angel's words to the shepherds. It reminds us that Jesus' birth was a gift from God, showing us His unstoppable love."

PRAYER

Dear God, Thank You for sending Your Son, Jesus, to earth as a baby. Thank You for Your unstoppable love. We pray that You will help us remember the true meaning of Christmas as we celebrate. Amen.

KID CONNECTION CONTINUES . . .

Small Group Leaders, use this time to continue to build community and learn more about your kids and their concerns. Listen closely so you are better equipped to pray for and reach out to each child.

SAY, "Tell us about the best Christmas you've ever celebrated. What made it so great? What is your favorite kind of food to eat at Christmas?"

Unit 1: God's Unstoppable Love

The Littlest Shepherd

Challenge the children in your ministry this Winter Quarter as you present four of the 5-Gs: **Grace**, **Growth**, **Group**, and **Gift**. Unit 1 powerfully illustrates the **Group** and **Grace** "Gs" as Small Groups celebrate Christmas and kids hear about the "Unstoppable Love" God showed when He sent His Son, Jesus, to earth. In Unit 2, **Growth** and **Gift** are emphasized as kids learn from Jesus' example how to live "The Extreme Life." This quarter ends with Unit 3, "Show Me the Shepherd." Children will **Grow** as they explore how we are like sheep and Jesus is our Good Shepherd, and experience **Grace** when they hear the salvation message. Throughout the quarter, kids will learn more about what it means to "do life with God in the picture."

BIBLE SUMMARY

Luke 2:1-20; Matthew 1:18-25
Joseph and Mary had to travel from Nazareth to Bethlehem for the census. When they arrived, there was no place for them to stay, so they stayed in a stable. While they were there, Jesus was born. Mary wrapped Him in cloths and laid Him in a manger. Angels appeared to shepherds who were tending their sheep in the fields. The angels praised God and told the shepherds where to find the baby. The shepherds visited Him and were amazed.

KEY CONCEPT
We are never too little or too big to know God's unstoppable love at Christmas.

For today's lesson, children in Kindergarten through 5th Grade can be combined for the Large Group Program. During Large Group, children will watch a video called, "The Littlest Shepherd." This original, fictional story is about a little shepherd boy who learns he is not too little to be a part of the very first Christmas story. He learns that everyone—small or big—can be a part of God's plan if they keep their hearts open to God's unstoppable love for them.

BIBLE VERSE

"This is how God showed His love among us: He sent His one and only Son into the world." I John 4:9

OBJECTIVES

KNOW WHAT (LG): Children will watch a fictional story, "The Littlest Shepherd," which tells the story of the birth of Jesus as seen through the eyes of a little shepherd boy.
SO WHAT (LG): Children will learn that God, through His love, sent Jesus into the world and He wants everyone, young and old, to know Jesus.
NOW WHAT (SG): Children will participate in an activity to discover ways they can get to know Jesus.

SPIRITUAL FORMATION

Friendship/Knowledge

5-G

Growth/Group

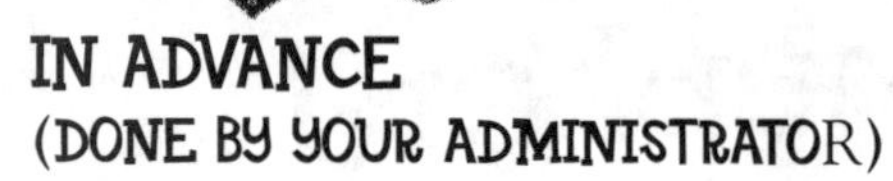

IN ADVANCE
(DONE BY YOUR ADMINISTRATOR)

- Photocopy and cut out the Question Cards—one set per group (pages 29-31 in *Administrator's Guidebook*).
- Gather mini marshmallows—approximately 30 per group.
- Gather toothpicks—approximately 60 per group.
- Photocopy and cut out the Bible Verse Cards—one per child (page 32 in *Administrator's Guidebook*).
- Place the above-mentioned items in a bin for each Small Group Leader.

LEADER'S PREP

When you were a child, did the month of December seem three times longer than any other month of the year? When we're children, often the closer Christmas gets, the slower time seems to pass. Christmas is special. Even as children we know this. Underneath the decorations and hoopla, kids often recognize there is something special about Christmas that makes it different from other holidays. Do you remember being amazed at the truth of God's grace when you first saw Christmas as a personal expression of love from God to you? When we think of Christmas this way, we celebrate the season as God intended. Read Luke 2:1-20 and Matthew 1:18-25. Do you feel a childlike anticipation as you wait for Christmas to arrive? Are you still awestruck when you sing out the truth in a Christmas carol you've sung hundreds of times before? Does your soul take delight in the story that is 2000 years old and yet new each time it is heard? With each passing year, allow yourself to be impacted anew by the Christmas message—and rejoice in your personal relationship with the One who was sent from heaven to save the world.

SHEPHERDING TIP
Be prepared to share about a time people thought you were too young for something at Christmas.

KID CONNECTION
(5 minutes)

WELCOME the kids to your Small Group.
ASK, "Are you excited about Christmas?"
SHARE about a time when people thought you were too young for certain activities at Christmas. (Examples: I was too young to get a moped for Christmas, too young to help my mom bake, to go Christmas caroling at night, to stay up really late on Christmas Eve.)
ASK, "What are some things you want to do at Christmas, but your parents or your teacher say you are too young?"
ASK, "What are you now old enough to do at Christmas that you couldn't do before?"

TRANSITION

SAY, "Today in Large Group, we're going to watch a video of the story, "The Littlest Shepherd," that will tell us what the first Christmas might have been like. Watch closely to see if the littlest shepherd was too little or too big for Christmas."

SMALL GROUP

(20 minutes)

REVIEW

ASK, "Was the littlest shepherd too little or too big for Christmas?" *(Neither; no one is too little or too big for Christmas.)*

ASK the following questions, giving kids a chance to respond after each one.

- Do you think you are too big to listen to the Christmas story? Why or why not?
- Do you think you are too little for presents? Why or why not?
- Do you think you are too little to sing Christmas carols to Jesus? Why or why not?

SAY, "Christmas is all about Jesus, whom God sent to show us His unstoppable love. God wants everyone—big and little—to know Jesus. So we are going to play a game that will help us remember ways that we can get to know Jesus better."

ACTIVITY: TOO LITTLE OR BIG FOR JESUS

The purpose of this activity is to help kids discover ways they can get to know Jesus better. As they answer questions about knowing Jesus, they will build a tower that will help them see that the more they grow in knowing know Jesus, the more their friendship with Him will grow.

SUPPLIES PROVIDED BY YOUR ADMINISTRATOR

- ❍ Question Cards
- ❍ Marshmallows
- ❍ Toothpicks

SET UP

PLACE all the toothpicks and marshmallows in the center of the group.

SHUFFLE the cards and place them in the center of the group.

MAKE a triangle-shaped base using three toothpicks and three marshmallows.

PLACE the base on the floor so the kids can build up from there.

INSTRUCTIONS

TELL the kids, "Our challenge today is to build together the biggest, strongest, coolest tower we can using these toothpicks and marshmallows. You will all take turns drawing a card, answering the question on the card, and then adding a part to the tower. Your card will tell you what piece you get to add to the tower. The more questions we answer, the taller our tower will grow. Our growing tower will remind us that the more we grow in knowing Jesus, the more our friendship with Him grows."

ASK, "Are you ready to build?"

FIND out who in the group has the birthday closest to Christmas and have that person go first.

CONTINUE going around the circle, having each child draw a card, answer the question on the card, and build part of the tower.

SHUFFLE the cards and continue building the tower if you get through all of the cards and have extra time.

WRAP-UP

SAY, "Wow! We built a great tower. We need to remember what this tower represents. Each question we answered helped us to think about ways we can get to know Jesus better. Each time we answered the question, we got to add more to our tower, which meant it grew bigger. This is how it works in our lives—the more we grow in knowing Jesus and the more we obey Him, the more our friendship with Him grows. Growing closer to Jesus means we begin to think and do things like Jesus would. Christmas is a great time to think about how we can grow in knowing Jesus better and better. God sent Jesus to us at Christmas to show us His unstoppable love, and He wants everyone to know Jesus. Remember, We are never too little or too big to know God's unstoppable love at Christmas."

BIBLE VERSE

SAY, "Today's Bible verse reminds us of God's unstoppable love, which He shows us through His Son, Jesus. The verse is I John 4:9 and it says, 'This is how God showed His love among us: He sent His one and only Son into the world.' "

GIVE each child a Bible Verse Card and repeat the verse together.

PRAYER

Dear God,

Thank You for all that each of these kids has learned about Jesus this year and how much they have grown. Please help all of us to know more about Your Son, Jesus, so we can grow to be more like Him. Amen.

KID CONNECTION CONTINUES . . .

Small Group Leaders, use this time to continue to build community and learn more about your kids and their concerns. Listen closely so you are better equipped to pray for and reach out to each child.

ASK, "If you were sixteen years old, what is one thing you would do for Jesus that you don't think you can do now?"

Unit 1: God's Unstoppable Love

Anna and Simeon

Challenge the children in your ministry this Winter Quarter as you present four of the 5-Gs: **Grace**, **Growth**, **Group**, and **Gift**. Unit 1 powerfully illustrates the **Group** and **Grace** "Gs" as Small Groups celebrate Christmas and kids hear about the "Unstoppable Love" God showed when He sent His Son, Jesus, to earth. In Unit 2, **Growth** and **Gift** are emphasized as kids learn from Jesus' example how to live "The Extreme Life." This quarter ends with Unit 3, "Show Me the Shepherd." Children will **Grow** as they explore how we are like sheep and Jesus is our Good Shepherd, and experience **Grace** when they hear the salvation message. Throughout the quarter, kids will learn more about what it means to "do life with God in the picture."

BIBLE SUMMARY

Luke 2:21-40

In this lesson, children will learn the story of Anna and Simeon. They will learn that Anna and Simeon remembered that God had promised a Savior, and they thanked God for keeping His promise and sending Jesus. Children will hear that Simeon held Jesus when He was presented at the temple as a baby. The children will have an opportunity to thank God for the things that He has given to them.

BIBLE VERSE

"Remember the wonders He has done." Psalm 105:5

OBJECTIVES

KNOW WHAT (LG): Children will hear the story of Anna and Simeon at the temple with baby Jesus.

SO WHAT (LG): Children will learn that God is good, and we can thank Him for what He has done.

NOW WHAT (SG): Children will participate in an activity to remember some of the good things God has done for them this past year and thank Him.

SPIRITUAL FORMATION

Thankfulness/Trust

5-G

Growth/Group

IN ADVANCE
(DONE BY YOUR ADMINISTRATOR)

- Photocopy and cut out Bible Verse Cards—one per child (page 33 in *Administrator's Guidebook*).
- Gather small pieces of paper—three per child.
- Collect paper bags—one per Small Group.
- Gather butcher paper—one large piece per Small Group.
- Collect markers—one set per Small Group.
- Place the above-mentioned items in a bin for each Small Group Leader.

LEADER'S PREP

Have you ever had a friend or family member tell you that they feel they have been taken for granted? Maybe they feel that you have ignored all that they have done for you or how they have served you. God is often who we take for granted the most. Every breath we take is a gift from Him. Every sunset we see He has orchestrated. Every time we walk in our home, we are experiencing a gift from Him. God has once again been faithful to you this year. How recently have you expressed your gratitude to Him? How often do you express your thankfulness to Him? This week think of all the ways God has been good to you this year. At the end of the week, take time to thank God specifically and thoroughly! He deserves to be celebrated.

KID CONNECTION

(5 minutes)

WELCOME the kids to your Small Group. **CONNECT** with your kids, asking them what they enjoyed most about Christmas. **ASK**, "Share about a time when someone thanked you for something. How did it make you feel?"

SAY, "It is so great to hear someone say 'thank you' and know that they appreciated something you did for them."

TRANSITION

SAY, "Today in Large Group, we are going to learn about two people named Anna and Simeon. Listen to find out why they were so thankful to God."

SMALL GROUP

(20 minutes)

REVIEW

ASK, "Why were Anna and Simeon thankful to God? *(God kept His promise to send Jesus to earth, they saw the baby Jesus, and Simeon held Jesus.)* How do you think they felt? Why?"

SAY, "Just like Anna and Simeon, we can say 'thank you' to God, too."

ACTIVITY: THANKFUL PICTIONARY®

The purpose of this activity is to give the children an opportunity to think of things they are thankful to God for and realize that everything they have comes from God. He loves them with an unstoppable, never-ending love.

SUPPLIES PROVIDED BY YOUR ADMINISTRATOR

- ❍ Small pieces of paper
- ❍ Paper bag
- ❍ Butcher paper
- ❍ Markers

SET UP

HAND three pieces of paper to each child.
LAY out the piece of butcher paper and markers.

SHEPHERDING TIP

During the Pictionary® game, have fun and let the ideas flow. Don't force a child to draw. If they don't feel comfortable drawing for the group or are unsure about their drawing skills, allow them to just participate in the rest of the game. When your group looks at all of the words and pictures on the paper, allow the children a moment to think about how big God's love really is for them.

INSTRUCTIONS

SAY, "Christmas is a wonderful time to remember and thank God for all the wonderful things He has done for us this past year, just like Anna and Simeon did. Today we are going to spend our Small Group Time playing a game that will help us remember what we can thank God for."

ASK, "Who has ever played the game Pictionary®? Today we are going to play a game that is like Pictionary®. Here's how it works."

SAY, "These pieces of paper are for you to write down three things you are thankful to God for. It is important for you to write down things that you can draw, because we will be using these ideas for our Pictionary® game."

TELL the children to write down one thing on each paper they are thankful for.

HAVE them fold the papers and put them in the paper bag.

EXPLAIN, "Now we are going to begin our Pictionary® game. To play, one person in the group will pick out a piece of paper from the bag and then draw the picture on this piece of butcher paper. The first person to guess the picture will be the next person to draw. When we finish, we will have an entire poster of all the ways God has shown His goodness to us."

CHOOSE someone in the group to go first.

HAVE him/her choose a piece of paper from the bag.

SHEPHERDING TIP

You may need to give children a few ideas of how to draw what is on the paper.

WRITE the word next to the picture after someone guesses the correct answer.

CONTINUE the game, guiding the children to draw their pictures in different places on the butcher paper, filling all the spaces.

SHEPHERDING TIP

If you find some duplicate words just put them aside and draw another word from the bag. If you are running out of time, read the rest of the slips of paper with the group and write them on the paper so that all words are represented.

HOLD up the butcher paper after the game is over.

SAY, "God has shown His unstoppable love for us in many ways. **WE CAN THANK GOD BECAUSE HIS UNSTOPPABLE LOVE IS FOR ALL TIME.**"

CONTINUE, "I am going to lay this butcher paper in the middle of our group and say a prayer of thanksgiving to God, just like Anna and Simeon. I will start by saying, 'God, I am thankful for my family.' Then anyone else who would like to can say thank You, too. You can finish this sentence, "Dear God, I am thankful for ________." You can use our "Thankful" paper to help you remember all the things for which we are thankful. Let's pray."

PRAY, "God, You are so good. We are thankful to You for so many things. Hear our prayers of thanksgiving. God, I am thankful for my family."

ALLOW the children to say their prayers of thanksgiving to God.

SHEPHERDING TIP

Make sure to leave enough silence so anyone still deciding to pray can, but don't leave too much time to distract the group. You know your group, so be sensitive to their uniqueness.

END the prayer by saying "Amen" when you think the group is done.

SAY, "You did a great job thanking God for His goodness. Let's take one more look at all of the ways God has shown His goodness to us."

HOLD up the butcher paper to see all the ways God has been good.

SAY, "Anna and Simeon thanked God for keeping His promises, and God keeps His promises to us as well."

WRAP-UP

SAY, "We learned that like Anna and Simeon, **WE CAN THANK GOD FOR HIS UNSTOPPABLE LOVE THAT IS FOR ALL TIME**. God's love is for all time—past, present, and future."

BIBLE VERSE

GIVE a Bible Verse Card to each child and repeat the verse together. "Remember the wonders He has done." Psalm 105:5

REMIND the kids, "Our verse today encourages us to thank God for His goodness. God really has been good to us this year, and I know He will be good to us in the future, too!"

PRAYER

Dear God,

Thank You for (*each child's name*) and the joy they bring to my life. We look forward to the new year and ask that You will help each of us to grow more and more in our friendship with You. Amen.

KID CONNECTION CONTINUES . . .

Small Group Leaders, use this time to continue to build community and learn more about your kids and their concerns. Listen closely so you are better equipped to pray for and reach out to each child.

SAY, "Tell us about one person you are thankful for and why."

ASK, "What is one thing you are looking forward to in the New Year?"

Unit 2 Overview

The Extreme Life

Unit Summary

The second unit of this Winter quarter teaches children about the "extreme" teachings of Jesus. His teachings were extreme because they went the extra mile beyond what was expected. Children will learn that by following Jesus' teachings, they can live their lives in extreme ways, which is the best way. In Lesson 6, children will learn that Jesus asks us to love others by loving our enemies and loving those who hurt us. In Lesson 7, through the story of the woman caught in adultery, they will learn that Jesus taught us to forgive in extreme ways. We must forgive for free, even when it is difficult. In Lesson 8, children will learn about extreme serving. We need to serve others as if we are serving Jesus, to serve just like He did, and to serve quietly, without asking for attention or reward. At the end of this unit, kids will understand what it means to follow Jesus' teachings in order to live an Extreme Life—the very best possible life.

Lesson Overviews

Lesson 6

Extreme Love
Matthew 5:38-48
Key Concept: Jesus wants us to love others in ways that are not always easy.
Bible Verse: "Love each other as I have loved you." John 15:12
Know What (LG): Children will hear Jesus' teaching on extreme love.
So What (LG): Children will learn that Jesus loves us and taught us to love others.
Now What (SG): Children will play a game where they will be challenged to show love to others in ways that are not always easy.
Spiritual Formation: Loving others
5-G: Growth/Group

Lesson 7

Extreme Forgiveness
John 8:1-11; Matthew 18:21-22
Key Concept: Jesus wants us to forgive without counting because we all need forgiveness.
Bible Verse: "Forgive as the Lord forgave you." Colossians 3:13
Know What (LG): Children will hear about Jesus showing mercy and forgiveness to a woman who was caught in sin and hear Jesus' teaching about forgiveness.
So What (LG): Children will learn that Jesus is merciful and forgives us.
Now What (SG): Children will do an activity to practice choosing to be merciful and forgiving when someone hurts them.
Spiritual Formation: Forgiveness/Mercy
5-G: Group/Growth

Lesson 8

Extreme Serving
Matthew 6:1-4
Key Concept: Jesus came to serve others and wants us to serve others, too.
Bible Verse: "Serve wholeheartedly, as if you were serving the Lord." Ephesians 6:7
Know What (LG): Children will hear Jesus' teaching about serving others without drawing attention to ourselves.
So What (LG): Children will learn that Jesus came to serve and He wants us to serve others.

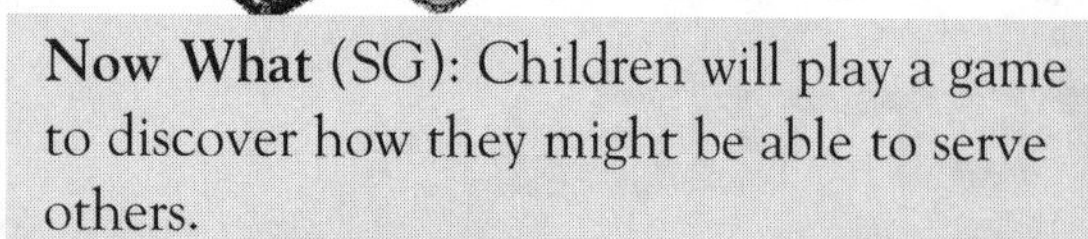

Now What (SG): Children will play a game to discover how they might be able to serve others.
Spiritual Formation: Serving
5-G: Gifts/Group

Large Group Presentation Summary

The Large Group presentations in this unit help kids understand Jesus' extreme teachings. Each week, the teacher begins by talking about what it means to be extreme. In Lesson 6, the Teacher reads the story directly from the Bible. In Lesson 7, the Teacher tells the story of the woman caught in adultery and a personal story about forgiveness. In Lesson 8, the Teacher interviews a church volunteer to help kids understand Extreme Serving. Each lesson ends with the "X Games" to help kids think about what they've learned, and how it applies to their lives.

Large Group Helpful Hints

1 Lesson 6 uses props to illustrate what it means to be extreme. If you don't have the props called for, feel free to use what you have on hand. For example, you could show a baby toy bat and a jumbo bat, or to be very simple, show a piece of paper versus a big roll of butcher paper.

2 Lesson 6 calls for three kids to participate in the drama. If you don't have a Drama Team already, take this opportunity to start building one. See information on this in the *Director's Notebook (pages 72-74)*.

3 Watch the wording of Lesson 7 very carefully as you tell the story of the woman caught in adultery. If kids have questions beyond what is provided in the lesson, encourage them to ask their parents.

4 In Lesson 7, you write "For Free" in black marker over a sign you have created. If you have more than one service and need to present the lesson more than once, consider making a small sign that says, "For Free," and hanging it over your big sign.

5 When choosing a volunteer to interview in Lesson 8, choose an outgoing, personable volunteer your kids are familiar with. It might be fun for them to see one of their very own Small Group Leaders on stage! Or, consider interviewing a kid in your ministry who volunteers in an area of the church.

Small Group Summary

In Small Group, kids will apply what they have learned in Large Group. Each activity in this unit is a car racing game. In Lesson 6, kids will answer questions about love, and be rewarded with a piece of race track. They put the pieces together to create a track on which they can race a toy car. In Lesson 7, kids race two cars against one another to see who will have the opportunity to answer a question. In Lesson 8, kids answer questions about Extreme Serving, then stick wax sticks onto posterboard to create a fun, curvy track. Then, they run the toy car on the track. These activities will help them understand what it means to live the Extreme Life.

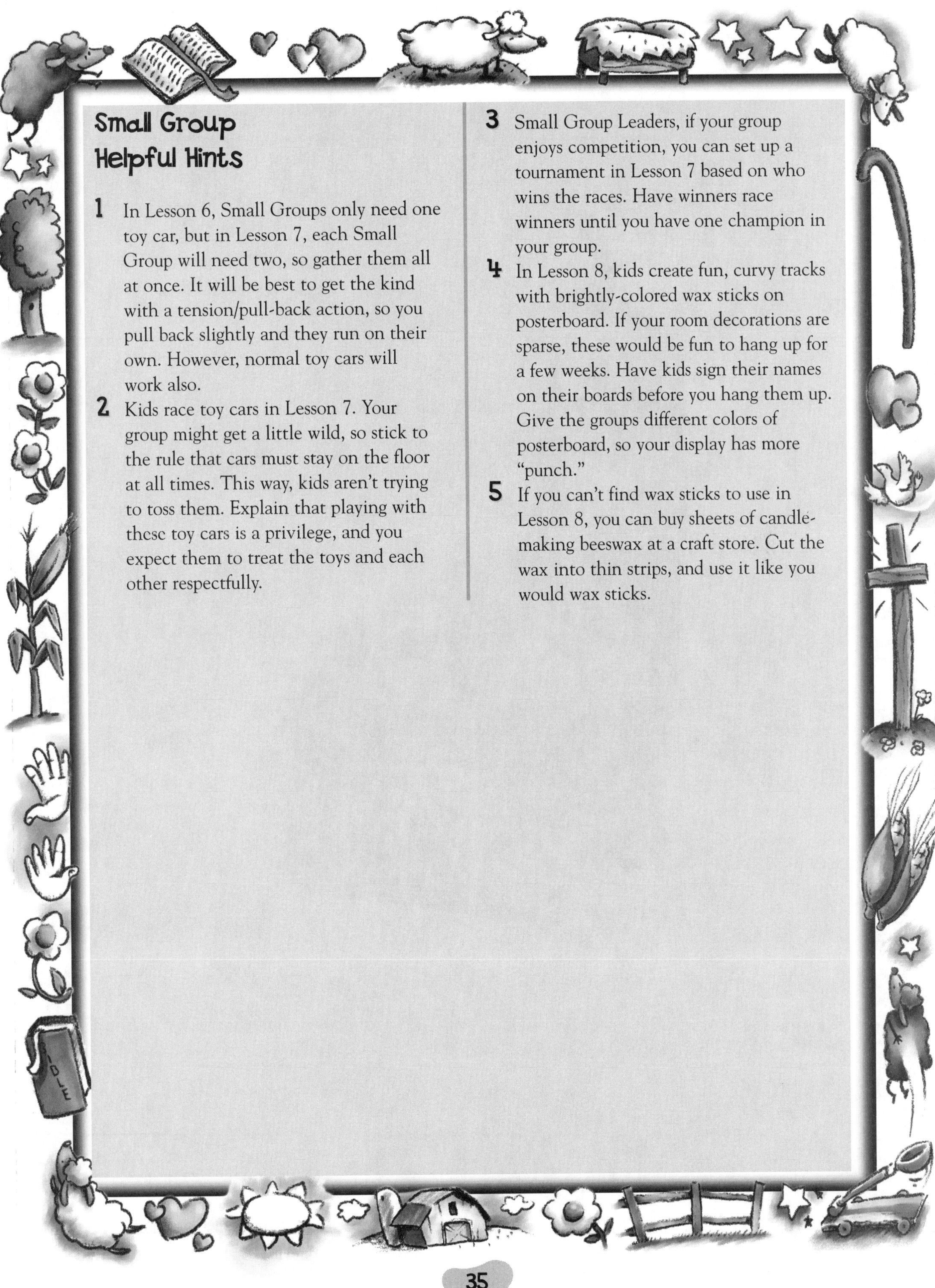

Small Group Helpful Hints

1. In Lesson 6, Small Groups only need one toy car, but in Lesson 7, each Small Group will need two, so gather them all at once. It will be best to get the kind with a tension/pull-back action, so you pull back slightly and they run on their own. However, normal toy cars will work also.
2. Kids race toy cars in Lesson 7. Your group might get a little wild, so stick to the rule that cars must stay on the floor at all times. This way, kids aren't trying to toss them. Explain that playing with these toy cars is a privilege, and you expect them to treat the toys and each other respectfully.
3. Small Group Leaders, if your group enjoys competition, you can set up a tournament in Lesson 7 based on who wins the races. Have winners race winners until you have one champion in your group.
4. In Lesson 8, kids create fun, curvy tracks with brightly-colored wax sticks on posterboard. If your room decorations are sparse, these would be fun to hang up for a few weeks. Have kids sign their names on their boards before you hang them up. Give the groups different colors of posterboard, so your display has more "punch."
5. If you can't find wax sticks to use in Lesson 8, you can buy sheets of candle-making beeswax at a craft store. Cut the wax into thin strips, and use it like you would wax sticks.

GOD'S SHEEP FOLD

Unit 2: The Extreme Life

Extreme Love

Challenge the children in your ministry this Winter Quarter as you present four of the 5-Gs: **Grace**, **Growth**, **Group**, and **Gift**. Unit 1 powerfully illustrates the **Group** and **Grace** "Gs" as Small Groups celebrate Christmas and kids hear about the "Unstoppable Love" God showed when He sent His Son, Jesus, to earth. In Unit 2, **Growth** and **Gift** are emphasized as kids learn from Jesus' example how to live "The Extreme Life." This quarter ends with Unit 3, "Show Me the Shepherd." Children will **Grow** as they explore how we are like sheep and Jesus is our Good Shepherd, and experience **Grace** when they hear the salvation message. Throughout the quarter, kids will learn more about what it means to "do life with God in the picture."

BIBLE SUMMARY

Matthew 5:38-48

Jesus taught us to live our lives in an extreme way. In this passage, Jesus is teaching about loving others. He says to go above and beyond what is expected of us, and to love our enemies and people who are difficult to love. He says that it is easy to love our friends, but we must love even those who persecute us.

KEY CONCEPT

Jesus wants us to love others in ways that are not always easy.

BIBLE VERSE

"Love each other as I have loved you."
John 15:12

OBJECTIVES

KNOW WHAT: (LG) Children will hear Jesus' teaching on extreme love.

SO WHAT: (LG) Children will learn that Jesus loves us and taught us to love others.

NOW WHAT: (SG) Children will play a game where they will be challenged to show love to others in ways that are not always easy.

SPIRITUAL FORMATION

Loving others

5-G

Growth/Group

IN ADVANCE

- Photocopy and cut out Bible Verse Cards—one per child (page 41 in *Administrator's Guidebook*).
- Photocopy Tracks onto cardstock and cut apart—two sets per group (pages 36-40 in *Administrator's Guidebook*).
- Photocopy Extreme Love Cards and cut apart—one set per group (pages 34-35 in *Administrator's Guidebook*).
- Gather toy cars—one per group. These should be the about the size of Hot Wheels® cars. Next week, you will need two cars per group, so you may want to gather them all at the same time.
- Gather tape—one roll per group.
- *Optional: Gather drinking straws—several per Small Group. Groups can tape these onto the race tracks to create side boundaries*

so cars don't fall off.

- Place the above-mentioned items in a bin for each Small Group Leader.

LEADER'S PREP

We throw the word "love" around so easily. "I love chocolate." "I love you; thanks for doing that for me." "I love that movie." Jesus was very clear about the concept of love. Not only did He teach love, but also, He demonstrated it. He chose to love us in spite of our sin. He modeled true love. His idea of love is not trite or sappy; it is real. It involves sacrifice and choice. Take some time this week to read Matthew 5:38-48. Take an inventory of your relationships. Do you demonstrate the extreme love Jesus teaches to those in your life? Do you love only people it is easy to love, or do you follow Jesus' word and love even your enemies? Jesus not only taught about extreme love, He modeled it. This week, try to follow His model by loving someone in your life who is difficult to love.

KID CONNECTION

(5 minutes)

WELCOME the kids to Promiseland.
ASK, "What did you enjoy most about your holiday season?"
ASK, "What does it mean for something to be extreme? *(It means something that goes above and beyond the ordinary.)* Do you know of anything that can be described as extreme? Why? What makes it extreme?"
SAY, "Jesus taught some things that were very extreme not only to the people who lived back then, but also to us today."

TRANSITION

SAY, "Today in Large Group, we are going to learn about some of Jesus' extreme teachings. Listen to find out what He teaches us about extreme love."

SMALL GROUP

(20 minutes)

REVIEW

ASK, "What does Jesus teach us about extreme love?" *(He teaches that extreme love means loving when it's hard, loving your enemies, and praying for those who hurt you.)*
SAY, "Jesus taught us and demonstrated extreme love in His own life. Jesus wants us to love others in ways that are not always easy."

ACTIVITY: EXTREME LOVE TEST TRACK

This activity will help children explore the difference between love and extreme love.

SUPPLIES PROVIDED BY YOUR ADMINISTRATOR

- ❍ Tracks
- ❍ Extreme Love Cards
- ❍ Toy Car
- ❍ Tape
- ❍ *Straws (optional)*

SHEPHERDING TIP

There are some questions that the children will have to answer from their own lives. Be aware of how they decide to show extreme love to these different people. This can be a wonderful way to get to know them in a new light as well as follow up with them later.

SET-UP

PLACE the Tracks, tape, and Extreme Love

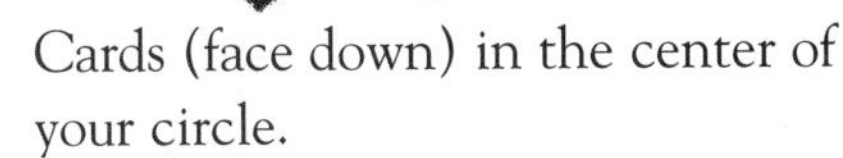

Cards (face down) in the center of your circle.

SAY, "We have learned a lot about how to live an extreme life, a life for God. Now, we are going to get a chance to see how we can demonstrate extreme love to those around us and have some fun, too. In this game, we are going to build a test track."

INSTRUCTIONS

SAY, "In this game, we will take turns drawing Extreme Love Cards. When it is your turn, pick up a card and answer the question. Each time you answer a question you will get a piece of track to build the test track. Here's the catch. Each question card tells you what kind of track you can take. It will say, straight, curved, tunnel or hill. Choose that section of the track, and tape it to the already existing track. When we are finished building, we will race our car on the test track!"

SHOW kids how to build the track by taping the ends together. To make the hill and the tunnel, fold on the dotted lines and attach to the track according to directions written on the track.

CHOOSE someone to go first and pick an Extreme Love Card and read it aloud. The group may help in answering the question. The child then picks up the kind of track designated on the card, and puts it in the center of the circle for the other children to play off of. Go around the circle until everyone has had a turn.

SAY, "That was fun. This track reminds me of how our life can be if we live life God's way. When we live life God's way, we are living an extreme life. It's a life with lots of curves and turns and lots of adventure. It is the best kind of life to live. Jesus called it the abundant life."

RACE the car along the track, giving everyone a chance as time permits. *Optional: If your Administrator has provided straws, tape them to the tracks as side boundaries so the car doesn't fall off as you race it.*

EXTREME LIFE CARD EXAMPLES:

How can you show love to your mom? How can you show extreme love? (curved)

How can you show love to your dad? How can you show extreme love? (S-curve)

Think of how you might show love at school to the person who is mean to you. What about extreme love? (tunnel)

Think of the most difficult person in your life. How could you show that person extreme love? (hill)

How could you show love to the person in school you don't get along with? How could you show extreme love? (curved)

How could you show love on your soccer team to the person who is hogging the ball? How can you show extreme love? (S-curve)

How could you show love to your brother or sister when they are mean to you? How could you show extreme love? (hill)

You are at home watching TV and your brother wants to watch his favorite show. You offer to tape the show for him to watch when you are done. Is that extreme love? Why? (straight)

Your mom isn't feeling well and she needs to clean the house. She asks you to help your little brother make his bed and clean up his room. What would be the loving response? What would be the extreme love response? (tunnel)

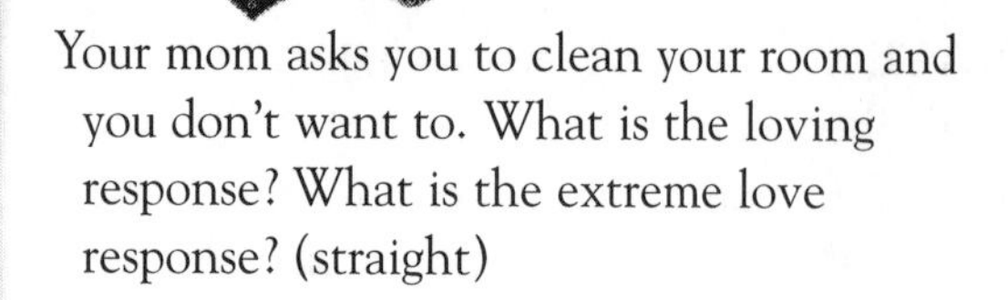

Your mom asks you to clean your room and you don't want to. What is the loving response? What is the extreme love response? (straight)

At recess, a kid who got you in trouble last week fell off the swing and landed in a mud puddle. How would you like to respond? What is the extreme love response? (straight)

Your little sister went in your room and ate some candy you had hidden. She now wants you to play a game with her. What do you want to do? What is the extreme love response? (tunnel)

What is one way to love someone, even when it is hard? (S-curve)

You are first in line to go out to recess, and you are so excited. You know your best friend has never been first before, so you decide to give up your place to him/her. Is that extreme love? Why or why not? (curved)

It is Christmas time and your family is going to buy some presents for a family who can't afford gifts. You think about giving some of your own money. What do you want to do? Would that be extreme love? (straight)

When has someone shown extreme love to you? (straight)

WRAP-UP

SAY, "Jesus' teachings were extreme. He taught us how to live extreme lives. Today we learned that extreme love means these three things: love your enemies, pray for the people who hurt you, and love people even when it's hard. **JESUS WANTS US TO LOVE OTHERS IN WAYS THAT ARE NOT ALWAYS EASY**. We can be people that show extreme love to others."

BIBLE VERSE

GIVE a Bible Verse Card to each child and repeat the verse together. "Love each other as I have loved you." John 15:12

REMIND the kids, "Our verse today reminds us how to love. God wants us to love others with the kind of love He has for us. Wow! We will need His help to do that. Let's pray!"

PRAYER

Dear God, Thank You for your extreme love for us. Thank You for the extreme teachings of Jesus, and thanks that You care enough about us to show us the best way to live. Help us to have extreme love for others this week. Amen.

KID CONNECTION CONTINUES . . .

Small Group Leaders, use this time to continue to build community and learn more about your kids and their concerns. Listen closely so you are better equipped to pray for and reach out to each child.

ASK, "Has anyone ever shown you extreme love? What did he/she do for you?"

Unit 2: The Extreme Life

Extreme Forgiveness

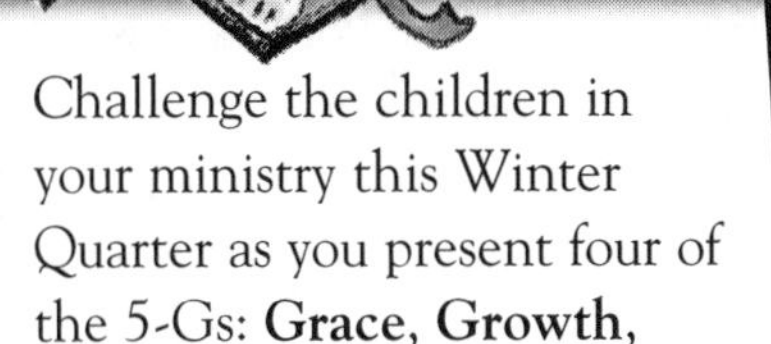

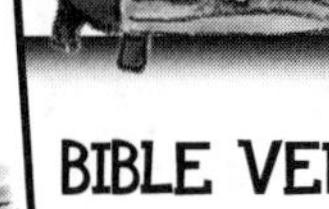

Challenge the children in your ministry this Winter Quarter as you present four of the 5-Gs: **Grace**, **Growth**, **Group**, and **Gift**. Unit 1 powerfully illustrates the **Group** and **Grace** "Gs" as Small Groups celebrate Christmas and kids hear about the "Unstoppable Love" God showed when He sent His Son, Jesus, to earth. In Unit 2, **Growth** and **Gift** are emphasized as kids learn from Jesus' example how to live "The Extreme Life." This quarter ends with Unit 3, "Show Me the Shepherd." Children will **Grow** as they explore how we are like sheep and Jesus is our Good Shepherd, and experience **Grace** when they hear the salvation message. Throughout the quarter, kids will learn more about what it means to "do life with God in the picture."

BIBLE SUMMARY

John 8:1-11; Matthew 18:21-22

The teachers of the law and the Pharisees brought a woman before Jesus. She had not been faithful to her husband, and they wanted to stone her as a punishment. Jesus just bent down, wrote in the dirt, and said, "If any one of you is without sin, let him be the first to throw a stone at her." The people left, one by one, until Jesus was alone with the woman. Jesus told her that she could go, and that she was to stop her lifestyle of sin.

KEY CONCEPT

Jesus wants us to forgive without counting because we all need forgiveness.

BIBLE VERSE

"Forgive as the Lord forgave you." Colossians 3:13

OBJECTIVES

KNOW WHAT: (LG) Children will hear about Jesus showing mercy and forgiveness to a woman who was caught in sin and hear Jesus' teaching about forgiveness.

SO WHAT (LG): Children will learn that Jesus is merciful and forgives us.

NOW WHAT (SG): Children will do an activity to practice choosing to be merciful and forgiving when someone hurts them.

SPIRITUAL FORMATION

Forgiveness/Mercy

5-G

Growth/Group

IN ADVANCE
(DONE BY YOUR ADMINISTRATOR)

- Photocopy and cut out Bible Verse Cards—one per child (page 44 in *Administrator's Guidebook*).
- Photocopy Extreme Forgiveness Cards and cut apart—one set per group (pages 42-43 in *Administrator's Guidebook*).
- Gather toy cars—two per group. These should be the about the size of Hot Wheels® cars. You will need these cars again next week, so collect them after the lesson.

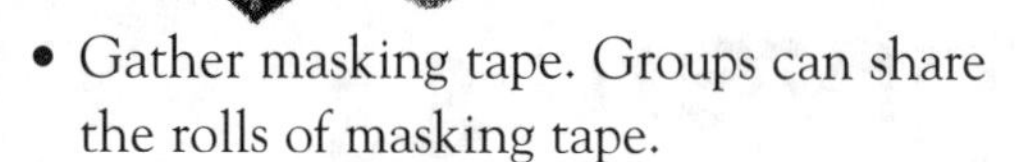

- Gather masking tape. Groups can share the rolls of masking tape.
- Place the above-mentioned items in a bin for each Small Group Leader.

LEADER'S PREP

Forgiveness can be incredibly difficult. Often, we feel justified in holding a grudge. We feel that someone has hurt us so badly, we can't possibly be expected to forgive. If someone hurts us over and over, it makes sense to finally stop forgiving him/her. But, read John 8:1-11 and Matthew 18:21-22. Jesus teaches us to forgive others. Not just once or twice. Not just if the person deserves it. He says to forgive seventy-times-seven. That seems crazy, impossible, and . . . EXTREME! But Jesus understood how important forgiveness is to us. Forgiveness can flush out bitterness and resentment and mend relationships. Do you have any relationships in which you need to exercise extreme forgiveness? Take the risk. Ask God to help you have the strength and courage to forgive. God can do amazing things in your life as a result.

KID CONNECTION

(5 minutes)

WELCOME the kids. Take a moment to connect with them.
SHARE a story with the children about a time when you needed to ask for forgiveness.
ASK, "Sometimes it is hard to say, 'I'm sorry.' When did you do something wrong and need to say you were sorry?"

TRANSITION

SAY, "Today in Large Group, we are going to learn about a woman in the Bible who needed forgiveness. To forgive is to give up bad feelings toward someone for something hurtful he or she did to you. It means to give up paying them back for how they hurt you. Listen to find out what Jesus did when He met her."

SMALL GROUP

(20 minutes)

REVIEW

ASK, "What did Jesus do when He met the woman caught in sin? *(Jesus forgave her for her sin.)* Who remembers what extreme forgiveness means?" *(Forgiving for free without counting)*
SAY, "Jesus showed us what extreme forgiveness looks like when He forgave the woman caught in sin. We have done things wrong and we need forgiveness, too. **JESUS WANTS US TO FORGIVE WITHOUT COUNTING BECAUSE WE ALL NEED FORGIVENESS.** Now, we're going to play a game where we can think about forgiveness in our own lives."

ACTIVITY: EXTREME FORGIVENESS RACE

The purpose of this activity is for kids to think about how they can show forgiveness in their own lives.

SUPPLIES PROVIDED BY YOUR ADMINISTRATOR

- ❍ Extreme Forgiveness Cards
- ❍ 2 Toy cars
- ❍ Masking Tape

SHEPHERDING TIP

Forgiveness can be hard for kids. They may have questions about particular situations in their own lives. Be sensitive to those questions. If you feel you can't give an answer to a particular situation, feel free to tell them that you will think about it and get back to them.

SET-UP

SIT in a circle with your group.
SET Extreme Forgiveness Cards face down in the center of your group.
CLEAR an area on the floor where you can race the two cars.
PUT a piece of masking tape on the floor as your starting line.

INSTRUCTIONS

SAY, "We are going to play a racing game. First, I'll pair you up with someone else. When it is your turn, you will both get a car. You will race the car from anywhere behind the starting line. If your car goes furthest, you get to answer the question. If you need help, you can ask the person you raced against. There is one catch: your car must be on the ground at all times. If all four wheels of your car are not on the ground, you automatically lose. You need to push it to go far, but you can't throw it."
PAIR up the children.
CHOOSE a pair to go first, give them both a car, and have them position their cars behind the starting line.
SAY, "Go!" and have them race their cars.
CHOOSE an Extreme Forgiveness Card and read the winner a question.
CONTINUE around the circle until everyone has had a chance to answer a question, until the cards are gone, or until you run out of time.

EXTREME CARD QUESTIONS (WITH NOTES AND ANSWERS)

1. Your brother borrowed your favorite CD and broke it. You are very angry. You want to secretly take one of his CDs. How could you show extreme forgiveness?
2. A friend talked about you behind your back last week and you have the opportunity to get him or her back. How would you handle the situation?
3. You have a friend who borrowed something of yours and broke it. He wants to borrow something else. What do you do? *(This is a very important question to discuss with the children. We want to make sure children realize that forgiveness does not mean that we keep putting ourselves in a position to be continuously hurt or used. In this situation, a child can forgive the other person and still choose not to lend something to that person again.)*
4. You have the opportunity to tell on your brother because he spilled something on the carpet. He always tells on you. How could you show forgiveness?
5. What is extreme forgiveness? *(Forgiving for free without counting)*
6. How hard is it for you to forgive someone who has hurt you? How can you learn to be a forgiving person? *(pray, read your Bible)*
7. Tell us about a time when you needed to be forgiven.
8. What do you find hard to forgive?
9. Your friend didn't invite you to her birthday party, and you feel very hurt. You were going to invite her to your birthday, but now you aren't sure. What do you do?
10. During soccer practice, your friend was hogging the ball and never passing it to you. You get the ball and you want to do the same thing. How could you fight those feelings?

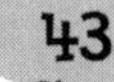

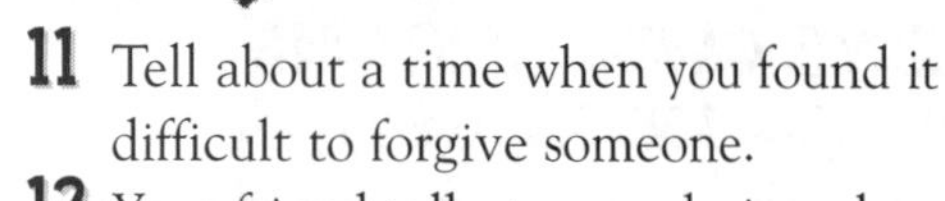

11 Tell about a time when you found it difficult to forgive someone.

12 Your friend talks to you during class, but your teacher notices you first. You get in trouble and have to sit on the bench at recess and your friend doesn't. You are angry, because it was really his fault. How could you handle the situation?

13 You are on the playground at school and one of the older kids comes over and takes something you are playing with. What do you do?

14 Your sister was listening on the phone when you were talking to your friends. You are mad at her and want to get her back. What do you do?

15 For what feels like the eighteenth time, your brother has played with your stuff without asking. How could you show extreme forgiveness?

16 Tell us about a time when you forgave someone else.

17 In today's story, who did the people bring before Jesus?

18 In today's story, when the people wanted to stone the woman caught in sin, what did Jesus tell them?

19 In today's story, why didn't people stone the woman?

20 Who are some people we don't have to forgive? *(Jesus tells us to forgive everyone without counting.)*

WRAP-UP

SAY, "Jesus taught us that by forgiving others, we can live extreme lives. Today we learned that **JESUS WANTS US TO FORGIVE WITHOUT COUNTING BECAUSE WE ALL NEED FORGIVENESS**. We can learn to be people that forgive others when we realize how much we need His forgiveness."

BIBLE VERSE

GIVE a Bible Verse Card to each child and repeat the verse together. "Forgive as the Lord forgave you." Colossians 3:13.

REMIND the kids, "This verse tells us that God wants us to forgive others with the kind of forgiveness He has for us. That is really difficult, so I'm glad we can ask Him to help us."

PRAYER

Dear God, Thank You for your forgiveness—we need it so much. This week, help us to forgive those around us without counting. Help us to forgive with Your extreme forgiveness. Amen.

KID CONNECTION CONTINUES . . .

Small Group Leaders, use this time to continue to build community and learn more about your kids and their concerns. Listen closely so you are better equipped to pray for and reach out to each child.

ASK, "Who is one person that you can work on forgiving this week?"

Unit 2: The Extreme Life

Extreme Serving

Challenge the children in your ministry this Winter Quarter as you present four of the 5-Gs: **Grace**, **Growth**, **Group**, and **Gift**. Unit 1 powerfully illustrates the **Group** and **Grace** "Gs" as Small Groups celebrate Christmas and kids hear about the "Unstoppable Love" God showed when He sent His Son, Jesus, to earth. In Unit 2, **Growth** and **Gift** are emphasized as kids learn from Jesus' example how to live "The Extreme Life." This quarter ends with Unit 3, "Show Me the Shepherd." Children will **Grow** as they explore how we are like sheep and Jesus is our Good Shepherd, and experience **Grace** when they hear the salvation message. Throughout the quarter, kids will learn more about what it means to "do life with God in the picture."

BIBLE SUMMARY

Matthew 6:1-4

Jesus taught about serving. He said to do your serving in secret, not in a prideful, showy way. He said we should not trumpet giving and serving before other people, but we should serve others without worrying about getting attention or reward. Jesus said that when we serve the needy discreetly, "your Father, who sees what is done in secret, will reward you."

KEY CONCEPT

Jesus came to serve others and wants us to serve others, too.

BIBLE VERSE

"Serve wholeheartedly, as if you were serving the Lord." Ephesians 6:7

OBJECTIVES

KNOW WHAT (LG): Children will hear Jesus' teaching about serving others without drawing attention to ourselves.

SO WHAT (LG): Children will learn that Jesus came to serve and He wants us to serve others.

NOW WHAT (LG): Children will play a game to discover how they might be able to serve others.

SPIRITUAL FORMATION

Serving

5-G

Gifts/Group

IN ADVANCE

(DONE BY YOUR ADMINISTRATOR)

- Photocopy and cut out Bible Verse Cards—one per child (page 47 in *Administrator's Guidebook*).
- Photocopy Extreme Serving Cards and cut apart—one set per group (pages 45-46 in *Administrator's Guidebook*).
- Gather toy cars—one per group. These should be the about the size of Hot Wheels® cars.
- Gather posterboard—one piece per group.
- Gather wax sticks—1 stick per child. These are long, thin sticks of wax about the size of a drinking straw. These can be found in toy stores and craft stores, or on toy websites such as www.zainybrainy.com.

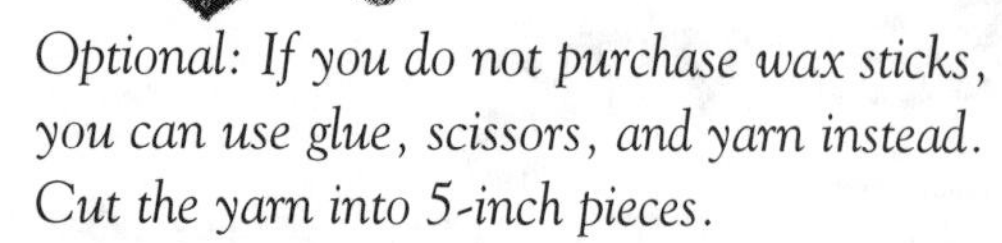

Optional: If you do not purchase wax sticks, you can use glue, scissors, and yarn instead. Cut the yarn into 5-inch pieces.

- Place the above-mentioned items in a bin for each Small Group Leader.

LEADER'S PREP

Read Matthew 6:1-4. You're in the middle of a difficult situation: you can serve someone, or you can walk away. No one will ever know either way. What do you do? Jesus teaches us to serve as if we are serving Him, to be a servant because He is a servant, and to serve without bragging or seeking attention. He taught and performed extreme service. Those moments are sometimes too infrequent in our lives. Often we find ourselves thinking how our actions are viewed by those around us, or what kind of credit we can get for doing them. Jesus' extreme teaching gives us perspective. He helps us understand how much He loves our acts of service. You might take some time this week to serve someone you normally wouldn't serve. Pay attention to your soul and your heart during those times. How do you feel? During those times, take a moment to sense God's pleasure, too.

KID CONNECTION

(5 minutes)

WELCOME the kids. Take a few minutes to find out if they have any news.

ASK, "Tell us about a chore that you do around your house. Do you get an allowance for that chore? What is a chore you don't get paid for?"

SAY, "When we do chores around the house, we are serving others. Jesus teaches to serve others even when we don't get a reward."

TRANSITION

SAY, "Today in Large Group, we are going to learn what Jesus teaches about extreme serving. Listen to find out what He teaches us about how to show extreme serving."

SMALL GROUP

(20 minutes)

REVIEW

ASK, "What did Jesus teach us about extreme serving?" *(Serve as if we are serving Jesus, be a servant like Jesus was, serve without bragging.)*

SAY, "Jesus showed us what extreme serving looks like. Jesus came to serve others and wants us to serve others, too. For the last two weeks, we have learned a lot about the extreme life, including extreme love, extreme forgiveness, and today, extreme serving. Now we are going to get a chance to see how we can demonstrate extreme serving to those around us and have some fun, too."

ACTIVITY: CURVE TRACK

The purpose of this activity is for kids to think more about what it means to serve others in extreme ways.

SUPPLIES PROVIDED BY YOUR ADMINISTRATOR

- ❍ Wax sticks
- ❍ Toy cars
- ❍ Extreme Serving Cards

SET-UP

SIT in a circle with your group.
PLACE the posterboard, toy car, and Extreme Serving Cards (face down) in the middle of the circle.
GIVE a wax stick to each child.
BREAK the wax sticks in half. Have kids put the wax sticks on the floor so they are not distracted as they continue learning how to play the game.

INSTRUCTIONS

SAY, "Today we are going to play a game called Curve Track. When it is your turn, you will choose an Extreme Serving Card. After you answer the question, you will bend one of your wax sticks into a crazy shape. You need to connect one end of the stick to the already-existing track, and leave the other end open, so another wax stick can be attached to it. Press the stick onto the posterboard to create a track. We will create a single-file line of wax sticks across the posterboard. Our goal is to create a track from the bottom, left corner to the top, right corner of the posterboard. When our track is finished, we will race our car on our track."
CHOOSE the person who has the most pets to go first. Have him/her choose a card, answer the question, and put down the first wax stick in the bottom left corner of the posterboard.
CONTINUE around the board until everyone has had a turn. If you run out of space on your posterboard, take off the wax sticks and start over. If you run out of cards, shuffle them and start over.
RACE the car on the track when you're finished. Allow each child a turn as time permits. If you finish with the entire lesson, feel free to take the track apart and build it again with your group.

EXTREME SERVING CARD QUESTION EXAMPLES

What is one way you could serve around your house? How can you make that extreme serving?

What is one way you could serve your brother or sister? How can you make that extreme serving?

What is one way you could serve your dad? How can you make that extreme serving?

What is one way you could serve your mom? How can you make that extreme serving?

What is one way you could serve the teammates on your sports team? How can you make that extreme serving?

What is one way you could serve a friend at school? How can you make that extreme serving?

Who do you find hard to serve? Why?

What is one way you could serve at your church?

What is one way you could help your parents by serving outside in the yard?

You clean up your room and the bathroom without your mom asking you to do it. Is that extreme serving? Why or why not?

Your mom is running late in the morning. What is an extreme serving thing you could do for her?

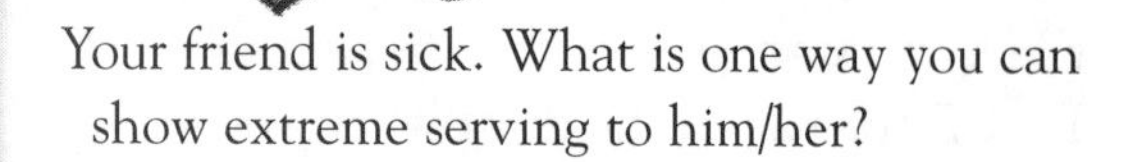

Your friend is sick. What is one way you can show extreme serving to him/her?

What is one thing you are good at? How could you use it to serve others?

You just sat down to play with the toys you got for your birthday. Your brother sits down next to you. What could you do to show extreme serving?

Your entire family has to spend Saturday cleaning the house. You complain and put it off, but get your part done. Is that extreme serving? Why or why not?

Your family just got home from a trip. What is one way you could serve them?

WRAP-UP

SAY, "Jesus taught us that by serving others we can live the extreme life. I know that is the kind of life that I want. **JESUS CAME TO SERVE OTHERS AND WANTS US TO SERVE OTHERS TOO.**"

BIBLE VERSE

GIVE a Bible Verse Card to each child and repeat the verse together. "Serve wholeheartedly, as if you were serving the Lord." Ephesians 6:7

REMIND the kids, "This verse tells us that when we serve, we should act as if we're serving Jesus by what we're doing."

PRAYER

Dear God, Thank You for showing us extreme serving. Please help us to serve others in extreme ways. Help us to not be concerned about getting rewards or attention for serving. Amen.

KID CONNECTION CONTINUES . . .

Small Group Leaders, use this time to continue to build community and learn more about your kids and their concerns. Listen closely so you are better equipped to pray for and reach out to each child.

ASK, "When did someone do something really nice to serve you?"

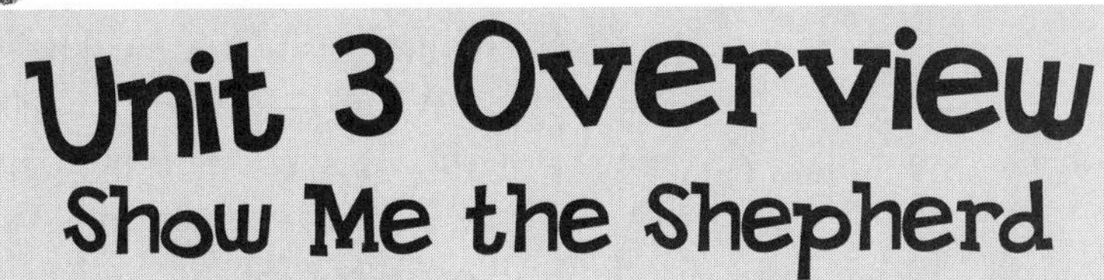

Unit 3 Overview
Show Me the Shepherd

Unit Summary

The third unit of this Winter Quarter teaches children about Jesus, the Good Shepherd. With a focus on the **GROWTH** and **GROUP** Gs, the children will be learning that we are like sheep, and we need Jesus, our Good Shepherd. Throughout the unit, the children will learn different characteristics of sheep and shepherds. In Lesson 9, children will learn that we are like sheep, so we need Jesus, the Good Shepherd. In Lesson 10, they will find out that like sheep, we are sometimes afraid, and the Good Shepherd knows how to comfort and care for us. Lesson 11 teaches kids the difference between needs and wants, and they will learn that the Good Shepherd meets our needs. In Lesson 12, they will hear that like sheep, we go astray, and Jesus sets limits and gives us guidance. This unit concludes with a salvation message. Lesson 13 focuses on **GRACE**, as kids learn that the Good Shepherd laid down His life for us, His sheep.

Lesson Overviews

Lesson 9

We, Like Sheep, Need A Shepherd
Psalm 23:1; John 10:11; Romans 7:18
Key Concept: We are like sheep who need Jesus, the Good Shepherd.
Bible Verse: "The Lord is my shepherd." Psalm 23:1
Know What (LG): Children will hear about how people are like sheep and Jesus is our Good Shepherd.
So What (LG): Children will learn that Jesus is the Good Shepherd and He can meet all our needs.
Now What (SG): Children will do an activity to personally identify ways they are like sheep and how they can follow the Good Shepherd.
Spiritual Formation: Dependence
5-G: Group/Growth

Lesson 10

We, Like Sheep, are Afraid
Psalm 23:2, 4; John 10:27, 29; Matthew 28:20
Key Concept: We, like sheep, are afraid and need Jesus the Good Shepherd to comfort us.
Bible Verse: "I will fear no evil, for you are with me. Your rod and staff comfort me." Psalm 23:4
Know What (LG): Children will hear how a shepherd cares for and comforts his sheep when they are afraid and focus on how Jesus is our Good Shepherd.
So What (LG): Children will learn that Jesus is the Good Shepherd and He will comfort us when we are afraid.
Now What (SG): Children will do an activity to identify ways they can trust Jesus, the Good Shepherd, when they are afraid.
Spiritual Formation: Trust
5-G: Growth/Group

Lesson 11

The Good Shepherd Meets Needs
Psalm 23:1, 3; Proverbs 2:8; Matthew 6:25-33; Philippians 4:19
Key Concept: Jesus, the Good Shepherd, knows our needs and can take care of us.
Bible Verse: "The Lord is my shepherd. He gives me everything I need." Psalm 23:1 (*NIrV*)
Know What (LG): Children will hear how a shepherd meets the needs of his sheep and hear how Jesus meets our needs.
So What (LG): Children will learn that Jesus, our Good Shepherd, will give us what we need.
Now What (SG): Children will do an activity to discover the difference between needs and wants and thank God for meeting their needs.
Spiritual Formation: Trust/Thanksgiving
5-G: Growth/Group

Lesson 12

We, Like Sheep, Have Gone Astray
Isaiah 53:6, Psalm 23:6, Matthew 6:19, Philippians 4:8
Key Concept: We, like sheep, go astray so Jesus, the Good Shepherd, sets limits.
Bible Verse: "All we like sheep have gone astray." Isaiah 53:6
Know What (LG): Children will hear how sheep tend to wander off and how a shepherd sets limits. The result of staying within the limits is that we will be safe.
So What (LG): Children will learn that Jesus, our Good Shepherd, has set limits in the Bible to keep us from going astray.
Now What (SG): Children will do an activity to explore the benefits of staying within the limits Jesus has set in the Bible.
Spiritual Formation: Study Scriptures/Obedience
5-G: Growth/Group

Lesson 13

The Good Shepherd Laid Down His Life for the Sheep
Isaiah 53:6; John 3:16; 10:11-16, 25-28
Key Concept: Jesus, the Good Shepherd, laid down His life for us, His sheep.
Bible Verse: "The Good Shepherd lays down His life for the sheep." John 10:11
Know What (LG): Children will hear that Jesus is the Good Shepherd who laid down His life for us, His sheep.
So What (LG): Children will learn that Jesus died to take the punishment for our sins and give us eternal life.
Now What (SG): Children will hear stories from Small Group Leaders who have admitted they have gone astray (sinned), believed that Jesus, the Good Shepherd, took the punishment for their sin, and have chosen to follow Him.
Spiritual Formation: Salvation
5-G: Grace/Group

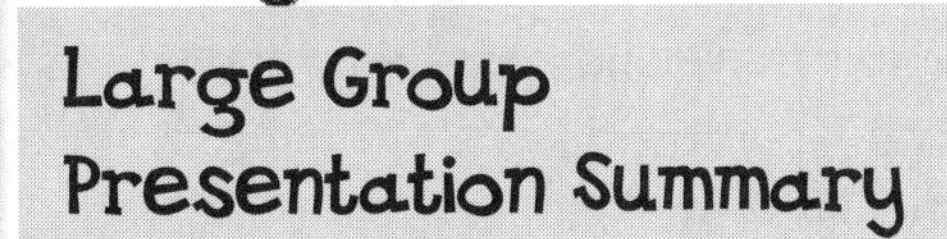

Large Group Presentation Summary

In this unit, a video entitled, *Show Me the Shepherd* introduces kids to the concept that we are like sheep and need Jesus, the Good Shepherd. In the video, "Bob the Sheep Expert" interviews sheep and a sheep farmer to find out information about sheep. Bob talks about how we are like sheep, and why we need a shepherd. This video aids the Teacher in helping kids absorb a lot of information quickly. The 5-G *Challenge Bible Dramas* video is used in Lessons 10 and 11 to help kids think about "Fear" and "Needs and Wants." Lesson 13 uses a set of props to teach kids the salvation message.

Large Group Helpful Hints

1. Throughout this unit, the Teacher can dress as if he/she works as a sheep farmer—jeans, hat, work boots.
2. To decorate for this unit, you could buy clip art books and enlarge clip art of farm objects. If you live in a farming community, ask a farmer if you can borrow bales of hay, corn stalks, or other farm materials.
3. To enhance the game in Lesson 9, get a sound effect CD in order to play "winner" noises and "sheep" noises during the game, have the kids wear costume sheep ears and noses when they get the signs around their necks and/or have the movie theater ticket taker and Sean's mom come onto the scene live and say their lines, instead of reading from an "official document."
4. To help illustrate Lesson 10, bring a shepherd's rod and staff to show the kids.
5. If you choose to do the Lesson 10 and 11 dramas live, watch the video for set and blocking techniques.
6. When you are teaching the Limit Signs in Lesson 12, increase audience participation by asking the kids to think of reasons to stay within the limits. For example, "What might happen if you went outside of God's limits and disobeyed your parents?"
7. Lesson 13 suggests more elaborate props than usual. Modify the props to use what you have available to you. For example, you can use small tables or sturdy TV trays instead of rolling carts. Make the signs smaller if they are too large for your teaching area. Make a fence out of foam core instead of buying one at a garden store.

Small Group Summary

Throughout this unit, kids will play a series of games and activities to help them apply what they have learned in Large Group. In Lesson 9, they play a game in which they catapult sheep into pens to help them think about why we need Jesus, the Good Shepherd. "Battlesheep," a game based on the game Battleship® is played in Lesson 10. In Lesson 11, kids pair up to think about what they would need to survive if they were stranded on a desert island, helping them understand the difference between needs and wants. The Lesson 12 game, where teams move their sheep from the pasture to the sheep fold, will help kids remember they are safe within God's limits. Finally, in Lesson 13, kids will review the salvation message and hear their leaders' testimonies.

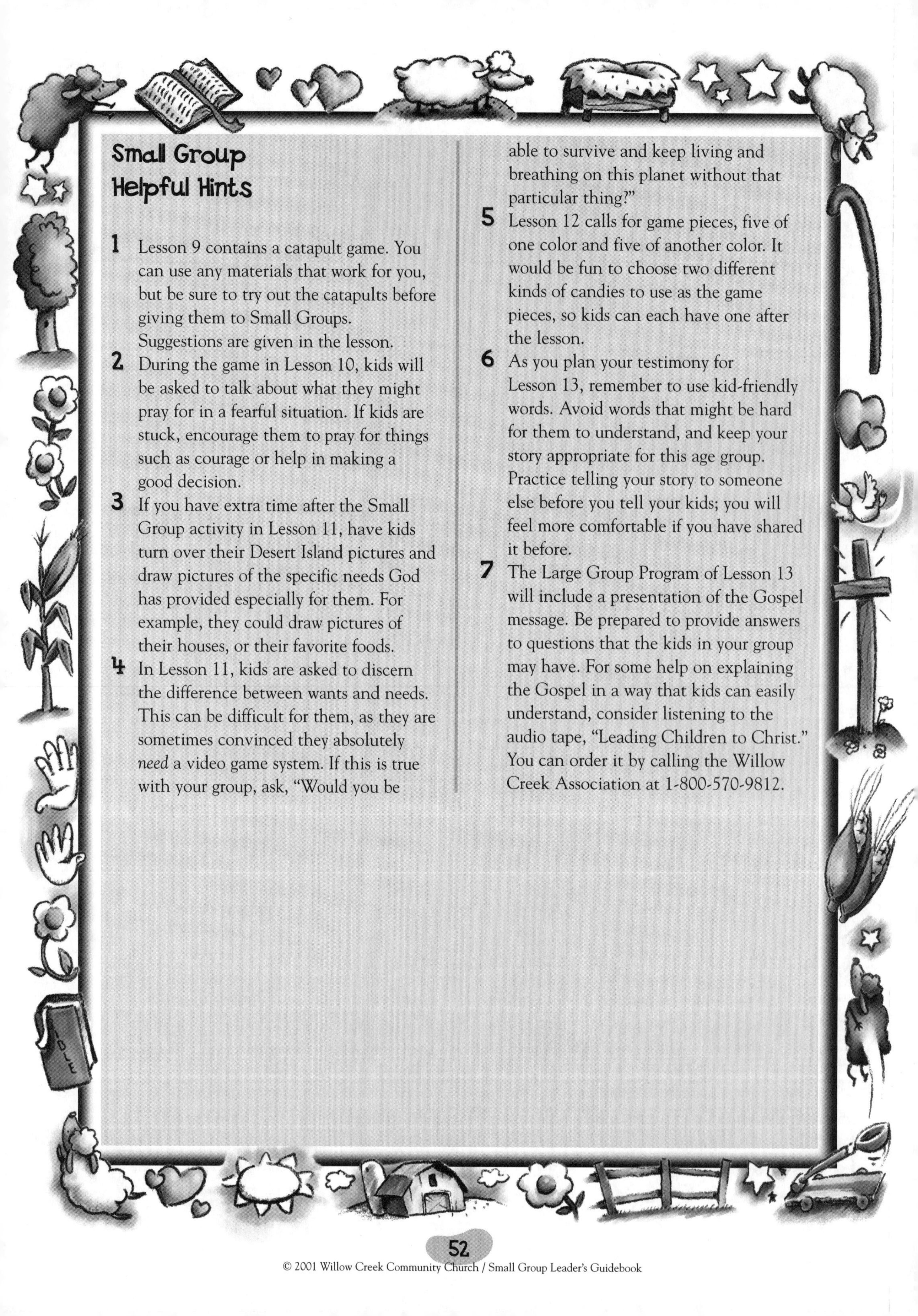

Small Group Helpful Hints

1. Lesson 9 contains a catapult game. You can use any materials that work for you, but be sure to try out the catapults before giving them to Small Groups. Suggestions are given in the lesson.
2. During the game in Lesson 10, kids will be asked to talk about what they might pray for in a fearful situation. If kids are stuck, encourage them to pray for things such as courage or help in making a good decision.
3. If you have extra time after the Small Group activity in Lesson 11, have kids turn over their Desert Island pictures and draw pictures of the specific needs God has provided especially for them. For example, they could draw pictures of their houses, or their favorite foods.
4. In Lesson 11, kids are asked to discern the difference between wants and needs. This can be difficult for them, as they are sometimes convinced they absolutely *need* a video game system. If this is true with your group, ask, "Would you be able to survive and keep living and breathing on this planet without that particular thing?"
5. Lesson 12 calls for game pieces, five of one color and five of another color. It would be fun to choose two different kinds of candies to use as the game pieces, so kids can each have one after the lesson.
6. As you plan your testimony for Lesson 13, remember to use kid-friendly words. Avoid words that might be hard for them to understand, and keep your story appropriate for this age group. Practice telling your story to someone else before you tell your kids; you will feel more comfortable if you have shared it before.
7. The Large Group Program of Lesson 13 will include a presentation of the Gospel message. Be prepared to provide answers to questions that the kids in your group may have. For some help on explaining the Gospel in a way that kids can easily understand, consider listening to the audio tape, "Leading Children to Christ." You can order it by calling the Willow Creek Association at 1-800-570-9812.

Unit 3: Show Me the Shepherd

We, Like Sheep, Need a Shepherd

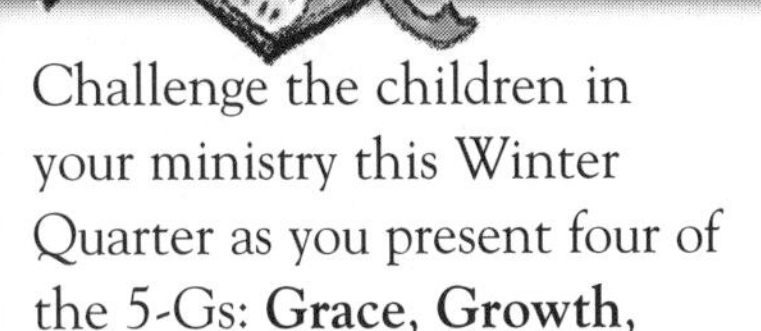

Challenge the children in your ministry this Winter Quarter as you present four of the 5-Gs: **Grace**, **Growth**, **Group**, and **Gift**. Unit 1 powerfully illustrates the **Group** and **Grace** "Gs" as Small Groups celebrate Christmas and kids hear about the "Unstoppable Love" God showed when He sent His Son, Jesus, to earth. In Unit 2, **Growth** and **Gift** are emphasized as kids learn from Jesus' example how to live "The Extreme Life." This quarter ends with Unit 3, "Show Me the Shepherd." Children will **Grow** as they explore how we are like sheep and Jesus is our Good Shepherd, and experience **Grace** when they hear the salvation message. Throughout the quarter, kids will learn more about what it means to "do life with God in the picture."

BIBLE SUMMARY

Psalm 23:1; John 10:11; Romans 7:18

The Old Testament says that God is our Shepherd, who cares for us so we have everything we need. In John 10:11, Jesus again uses the metaphor of the shepherd, saying He is our Good Shepherd, who gives His life for His sheep. In Romans 7:18, the Bible says we need a shepherd, because we are sinful people with sinful natures. We want to do what is good, but we sin. We need a shepherd to guide us.

KEY CONCEPT
We are like sheep who need Jesus, the Good Shepherd.

BIBLE VERSE

"The Lord is my shepherd."
Psalm 23:1

OBJECTIVES

KNOW WHAT (LG): Children will hear about how people are like sheep and Jesus is our Good Shepherd.
SO WHAT (LG): Children will learn that Jesus is the Good Shepherd and He will meet all our needs.
NOW WHAT (SG): Children will do an activity to personally identify ways they are like sheep and how they can follow the Good Shepherd.

SPIRITUAL FORMATION

Dependence

5-G

Group/Growth

IN ADVANCE

(DONE BY YOUR ADMINISTRATOR)

- Photocopy and cut out Bible Verse Cards—one per child (page 52 in *Administrator's Guidebook*).
- Photocopy and cut out Sheep Cards—one set per group (pages 49-50 in *Administrator's Guidebook*).
- Photocopy and cut out Score Cards—one per group (page 51 in *Administrator's Guidebook*).

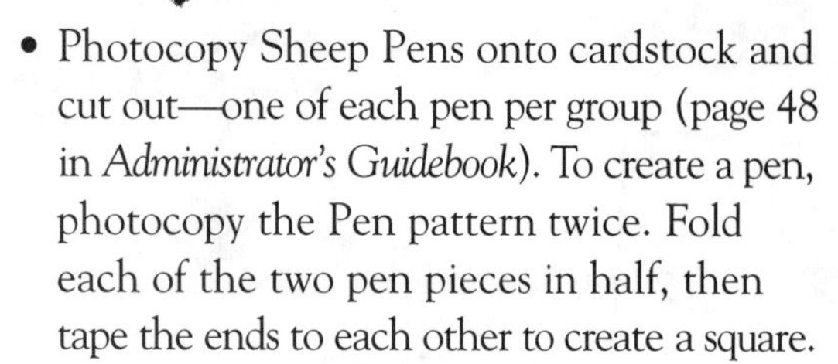

- Photocopy Sheep Pens onto cardstock and cut out—one of each pen per group (page 48 in *Administrator's Guidebook*). To create a pen, photocopy the Pen pattern twice. Fold each of the two pen pieces in half, then tape the ends to each other to create a square.
- Gather spoons (plastic or metal), thick markers, and sheep object—one of each per group. The sheep object can be a small sheep toy or eraser, or a cottonball attached to a paper clip, representing a sheep. Groups will put the Sheep object in the spoon, lay the spoon over the marker, and hit the end of the spoon to make the object fly into the Sheep Pens. Try out the catapult before giving the supplies to the leaders.
- Place the above-mentioned items in a bin for each Small Group Leader.

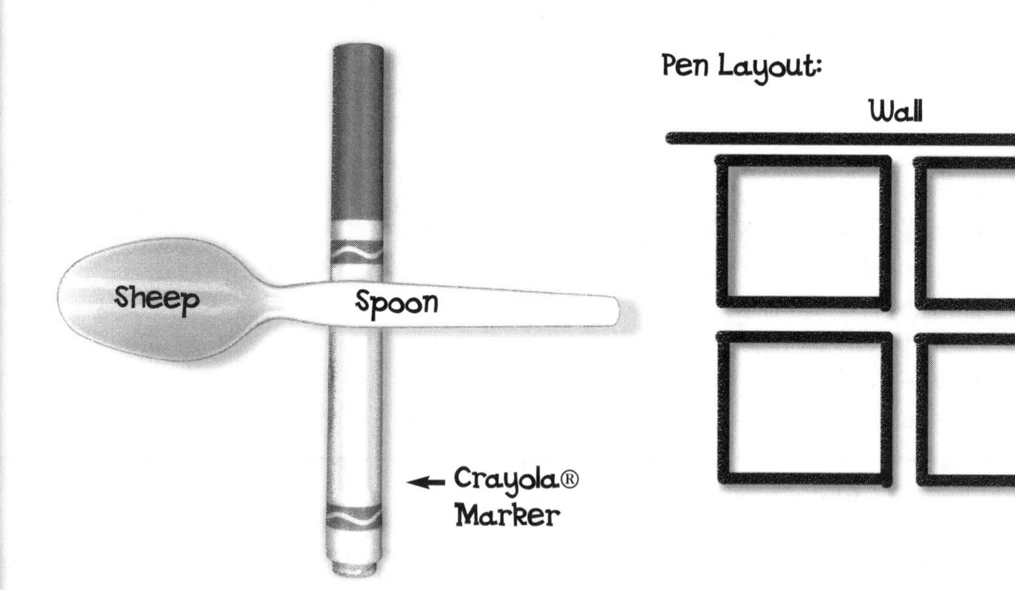

LEADER'S PREP

Read Psalm 23:1; John 10:11; and Romans 7:18. Are you really like a sheep? Take this little quiz to find out. Do little things make you anxious? Do you find that you tend to "follow the crowd" and make decisions based on what other people want versus thinking about what is right? Do you make unwise decisions, not always seeing the implications of those decisions? Do you sometimes feel you really can't make it on your own? If you answered "yes" to any of these questions, you need a shepherd! The truth is, we are all "sheep" who need a shepherd. It's a good thing that Jesus, the Good Shepherd, is available to us, always looking out for our best interests and caring for our needs. If we have a Shepherd we can depend on, why do we find it so hard to trust Him with our lives? Take some time this week to reflect on that thought. Ask God to help you recognize the areas of your life where you need the Good Shepherd and then remember that God will care for you like a shepherd cares for his sheep.

KID CONNECTION

(5 minutes)

WELCOME the kids to your Small Group.
ASK, "Can anyone tell me some facts about sheep? Let's list as many facts as we can."

TRANSITION

SAY, "Today in Large Group, we are going to learn some very interesting things about sheep. Listen to find out what sheep need most."

SMALL GROUP

(20 minutes)

REVIEW

ASK, "What do sheep need most? *(A shepherd)* Who is the Good Shepherd? *(Jesus)* Who remembers how we are like sheep?" *(We are clueless to danger, we follow the crowd, we are quick to panic, and we can't survive on our own.)*
SAY, "**WE ARE LIKE SHEEP WHO NEED JESUS, THE GOOD SHEPHERD.** We need Jesus to care for us because we don't always know how to take care of ourselves. Now we are going to get to play a game where we will discover how we, like sheep, need a shepherd."

ACTIVITY: CATAPULTING SHEEP

In this lesson, the children will begin to see that like sheep, they need the Good Shepherd, Jesus, to take care of them and guide them.

SUPPLIES PROVIDED BY YOUR ADMINISTRATOR

- ❍ Sheep Pens
- ❍ Sheep object (small object)
- ❍ Sheep Cards
- ❍ Spoon
- ❍ Thick marker
- ❍ Score Cards

SET-UP

SIT in a circle with your Small Group.
SET the four Sheep Pens up a few feet from your group.
ASSEMBLE the catapult to face the Sheep Pens. Lay the spoon across the marker, and put the sheep in the bowl of the spoon, as illustrated above.
PLACE the cards in a pile, face-down, in the middle of your group.

INSTRUCTIONS

POINT to the Sheep Pens and say, "These are the sheep pens. Each pen is marked with a different characteristic of sheep. The categories are: Follows the Crowd, Clueless to Danger, Quick to Panic, and Can't Survive on Their Own. We learned about these characteristics during Large Group."
SAY, "We are going to get a chance to see how we are like sheep as we play this game. Each card has a situation on it. After we read the card and decide which one of the four characteristics it is, we will try to catapult the sheep object into the correct pen. You will get three tries per turn. I'll show you how it works."

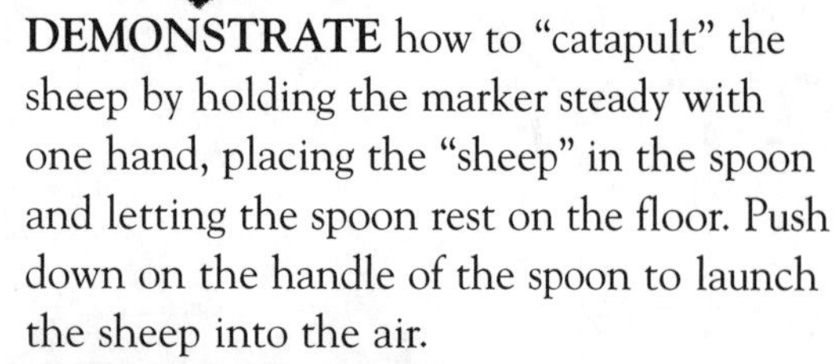

DEMONSTRATE how to "catapult" the sheep by holding the marker steady with one hand, placing the "sheep" in the spoon and letting the spoon rest on the floor. Push down on the handle of the spoon to launch the sheep into the air.

SHEPHERDING TIP
You may want to allow the children time to practice so they can see how to aim the catapult and judge the distance.

DIVIDE your group into two teams. Tell one team to sit on the right side of the sheep pens and the other team to sit on the left side. Leave room in front of the pens for team members to catapult the sheep.

SAY, "We will keep score. You will get 1 point for choosing the correct pen, and 1 point for catapulting the sheep into the correct pen. The team with the most points at the end of our time wins."

CHOOSE one team to go first. Direct the team to draw a card, read the situation, and decide in which pen the situation belongs (answers are listed below). Feel free to talk about the situations and put them in more than one category. If the team answers the question correctly, give them 1 point. Give a child three tries to catapult the sheep into the chosen pen. If the sheep lands in the correct pen, mark 1 point on the scorecard (2 points total). Retrieve the sheep and give it to the second team.

CONTINUE playing until all the situations have been answered or you run out of time.

SHEEP CARD QUESTION EXAMPLES

Follow the Crowd:

- Your friends all start talking about the new kid in your class. They are telling stories you know aren't true, but you join in anyway.
- You are at the video arcade and your friends want to play a violent video game. You go along because they pressure you to play.
- Your friend convinces you to sneak into your brother's room and take some of his video games.
- Your mom is at a meeting, and you are home alone with a friend. He/she convinces you to make prank phone calls, even though you know it is a mean thing to do.

Clueless to Danger:

- You ride your bike on a busy road by your house even though your parents told you not to.
- After school, you play with a group of kids when you know they break rules and make bad choices.
- You think that disobeying your parents is cool.
- You go to an Internet site and start chatting on-line with someone you don't know.
- You talk to a stranger at the park who keeps asking you questions.

Quick to Panic:

- You forgot your homework and worry all the way to school, thinking up stories of how you will explain it to your teacher.
- Your mom said she would pick you up after school and you're scared because you have been waiting for 10 minutes.
- You get separated from your family in the department store. You start to worry and run through the store.
- Your teacher announces book report partners, and you are paired up with the class bully. You are immediately scared!
- You move into a new house and are starting your first day of school. You're terrified because you don't have any friends.

Can't Survive on Their Own

- It's past your bedtime, and you just realized you didn't finish a homework assignment that is due tomorrow! You need help!
- You think your older brother might be smoking cigarettes, and you know smoking could really hurt him. You're not sure what to do. You need to ask someone for advice.
- You want to tell your friend not to talk bad about someone else, but you don't know what to say. You need someone else to help you figure it out.
- You saw your best friend looking at some one else's paper during a spelling test. You don't know whether to talk to him/her about this, and you need some advice.

WRAP-UP

SAY, "WE ARE LIKE SHEEP WHO NEED JESUS, THE GOOD SHEPHERD. How can you follow the Shepherd when you are in a situation where you are tempted to follow the crowd? *(Pray and ask God for courage.)* How can you follow the Shepherd when you are in a situation where you may feel worried and anxious? *(Pray, remember the Shepherd is with you.)* How can you follow the Shepherd when you are clueless to danger? *(Pray and remember what the Bible says.)* How can you follow the Shepherd when you need help?" *(Pray and ask God for help.)*

BIBLE VERSE

GIVE a Bible Verse Card to each child and repeat the verse together. "The Lord is my shepherd." Psalm 23:1

REMIND the kids, "This verse tells us that Jesus will lead us and guide us."

PRAYER

Dear God, Thank You for being our Good Shepherd. Please help us to remember that we can follow You, the Good Shepherd, and You will help us in all the situations we face. Help us to follow You this coming week. Amen.

KID CONNECTION CONTINUES . . .

Small Group Leaders, use this time to continue to build community and learn more about your kids and their concerns. Listen closely so you are better equipped to pray for and reach out to each child.

ASK, "What is one situation you have faced where you were tempted to follow the crowd? What happened?"

TWANG!
BYe
Wait! I've GoT one more nail!
Here, let me help ewe.
How sweet
Gifts
Okay, everybody in a straight Line!

Unit 3: Show Me the Shepherd

We, Like Sheep, Are Afraid

Challenge the children in your ministry this Winter Quarter as you present four of the 5-Gs: **Grace**, **Growth**, **Group**, and **Gift**. Unit 1 powerfully illustrates the **Group** and **Grace** "Gs" as Small Groups celebrate Christmas and kids hear about the "Unstoppable Love" God showed when He sent His Son, Jesus, to earth. In Unit 2, **Growth** and **Gift** are emphasized as kids learn from Jesus' example how to live "The Extreme Life." This quarter ends with Unit 3, "Show Me the Shepherd." Children will **Grow** as they explore how we are like sheep and Jesus is our Good Shepherd, and experience **Grace** when they hear the salvation message. Throughout the quarter, kids will learn more about what it means to "do life with God in the picture."

BIBLE STORY

Psalm 23:2, 4; John 10:27, 29; Matthew 28:20
Children will learn that we are easily frightened, just like sheep. They will learn that just like a Good Shepherd calms and comforts the sheep, Jesus, our Good Shepherd, knows how to calm and comfort us. He is always with us. Children will learn that no one can snatch them from Jesus' hand. They will identify ways they can trust Jesus when they are afraid.

KEY CONCEPT
We, like sheep, are afraid and need Jesus the Good Shepherd to comfort us.

BIBLE VERSE

"I will fear no evil, for you are with me. Your rod and staff comfort me." Psalm 23:4

OBJECTIVES

KNOW WHAT (LG): Children will hear how a shepherd cares for and comforts his sheep when they are afraid and focus on how Jesus is our Good Shepherd.
SO WHAT (LG): Children will learn that Jesus is the Good Shepherd and He will comfort us when we are afraid.
NOW WHAT (SG): Children will do an activity to identify ways they can trust Jesus, the Good Shepherd, when they are afraid.

SPIRITUAL FORMATION

Trust

5-G

Growth/Group

IN ADVANCE
(DONE BY YOUR ADMINISTRATOR)

- Photocopy and cut out Bible Verse Cards—one per child (page 58 in *Administrator's Guidebook*).
- Photocopy Battlesheep Grids and Opponent Grids—one of each per every two children (pages 53-54 in *Administrator's Guidebook*).
- Photocopy and cut out Fear Cards—one set per every four children (pages 56-57 in *Administrator's Guidebook*).

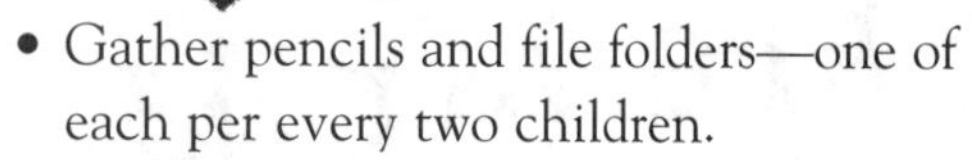

- Gather pencils and file folders—one of each per every two children.
- Photocopy Wolf Stickers onto return address labels—three stickers per every two children (page 55 in *Administrator's Guidebook*). You can purchase sheets of return address labels at office supply stores. (The template provided in the *Administrator's Guidebook* is created to accommodate Avery® Return Address labels, #5267™.) Or, you can photocopy the wolves onto sheets of solid sticker paper, then cut them apart.
- Place the above-mentioned items in a bin for each Small Group Leader.

LEADER'S PREP

Read Psalm 23:2, 4; John 10:27, 29; Matthew 28:20. How often does God tell us in scripture, "Don't be afraid?" It seems so often those phrases jump off the pages of scripture. Why? We are people prone to fear. We really are like sheep. One rabbit jumping out of the grass can send an entire flock of sheep into a panic. What do sheep do when they are scared? The entire flock runs. What calms the sheep? The presence of a shepherd. Isn't that true of us, too? When we know that God loves us completely and is able and willing to take care of us, why do we run in fear? Next time you are afraid, remember who you are. You are a child loved by a perfect heavenly Father who is able to calm and comfort you. You can rest in the safety of His arms. Trust the Good Shepherd: He's waiting for you to run to Him!

KID CONNECTION

(5 minutes)

WELCOME the kids to your group. **SHARE** an appropriate story of a time you were afraid. The goal is not to scare kids with your story, but to help them begin to think of a time when they were afraid.

ASK, "Tell us about a time when you were afraid. What happened?"

TRANSITION

SAY, "Today in Large Group, we are going to continue learning about sheep. Listen to find out one way we are like sheep."

SMALL GROUP

(20 minutes)

REVIEW

ASK, "In Large Group, how did we learn that we are like sheep? *(We are afraid.)* What helps sheep when they are afraid? *(The shepherd.)* What are two things you can remember when you are afraid?" *(Pray and ask Jesus for help, and remember that Jesus is with me all the time.)*

SAY, "**WE, LIKE SHEEP, ARE AFRAID AND NEED JESUS, THE GOOD SHEPHERD TO COMFORT US.** Now, we are going to get a chance to look at some of our own fears and see how we can defeat them. We are going to play a game where we can discover and overcome our fears."

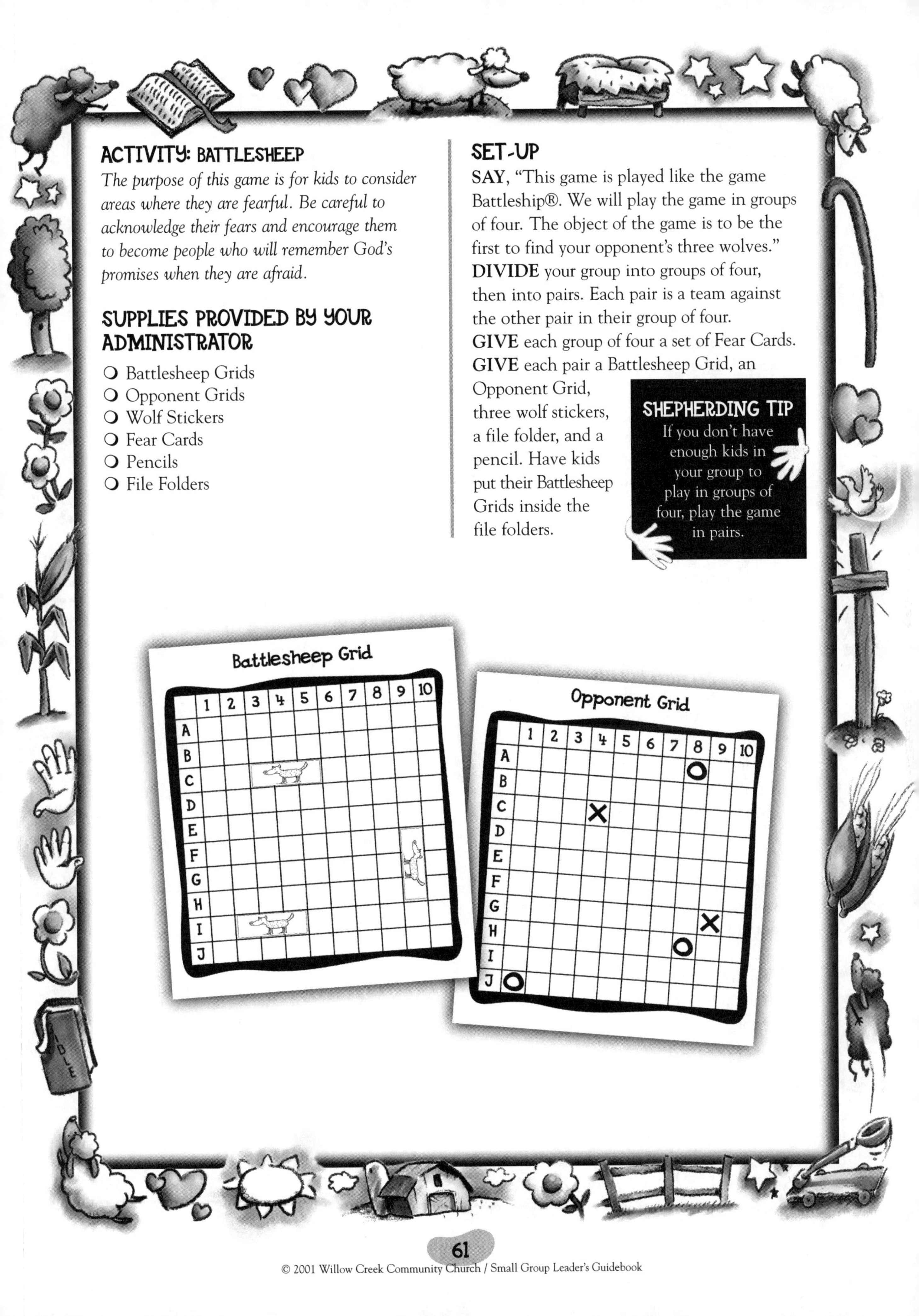

ACTIVITY: BATTLESHEEP

The purpose of this game is for kids to consider areas where they are fearful. Be careful to acknowledge their fears and encourage them to become people who will remember God's promises when they are afraid.

SUPPLIES PROVIDED BY YOUR ADMINISTRATOR

- ❍ Battlesheep Grids
- ❍ Opponent Grids
- ❍ Wolf Stickers
- ❍ Fear Cards
- ❍ Pencils
- ❍ File Folders

SET-UP

SAY, "This game is played like the game Battleship®. We will play the game in groups of four. The object of the game is to be the first to find your opponent's three wolves."
DIVIDE your group into groups of four, then into pairs. Each pair is a team against the other pair in their group of four.
GIVE each group of four a set of Fear Cards.
GIVE each pair a Battlesheep Grid, an Opponent Grid, three wolf stickers, a file folder, and a pencil. Have kids put their Battlesheep Grids inside the file folders.

SHEPHERDING TIP
If you don't have enough kids in your group to play in groups of four, play the game in pairs.

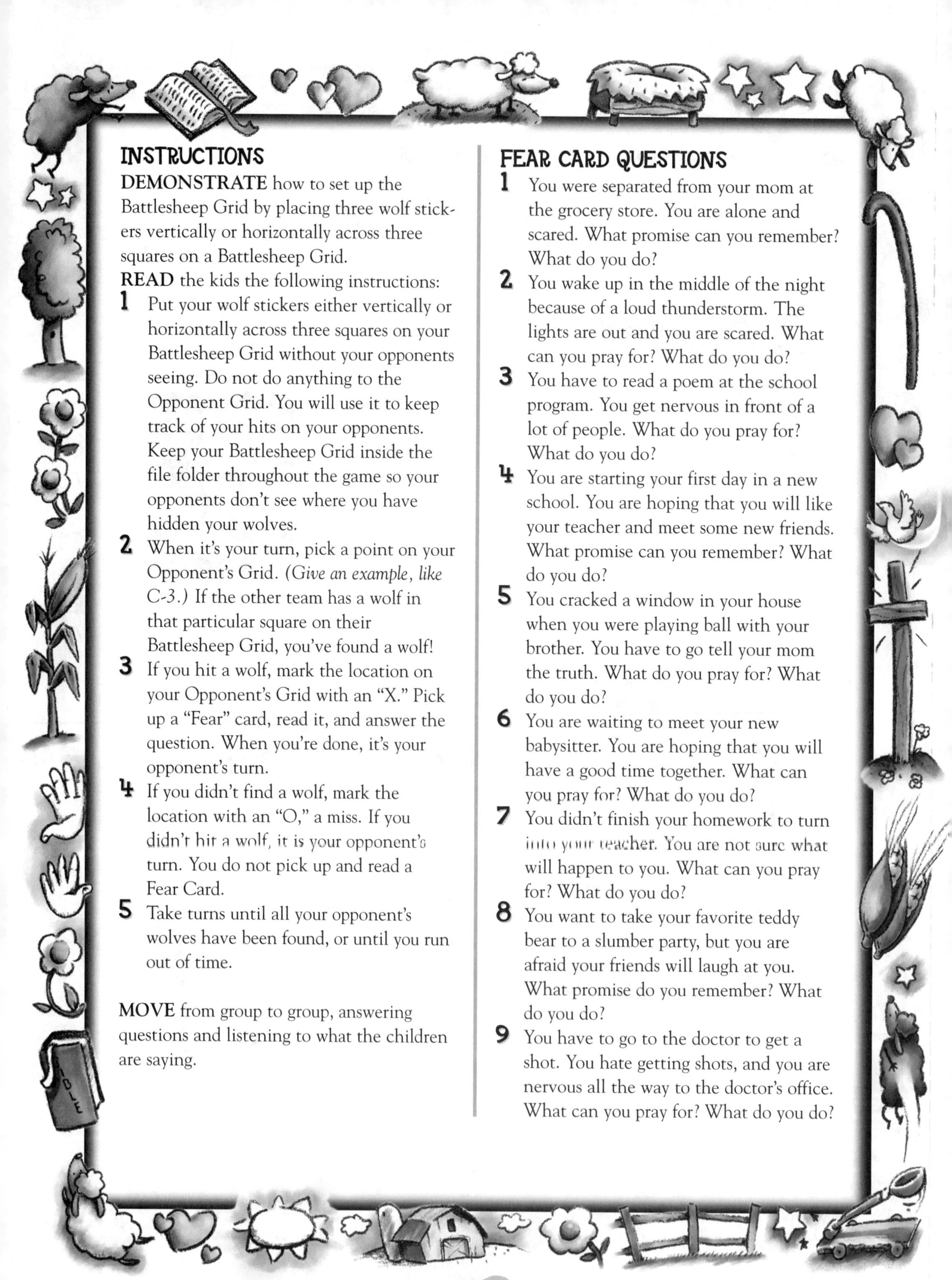

INSTRUCTIONS

DEMONSTRATE how to set up the Battlesheep Grid by placing three wolf stickers vertically or horizontally across three squares on a Battlesheep Grid.

READ the kids the following instructions:

1. Put your wolf stickers either vertically or horizontally across three squares on your Battlesheep Grid without your opponents seeing. Do not do anything to the Opponent Grid. You will use it to keep track of your hits on your opponents. Keep your Battlesheep Grid inside the file folder throughout the game so your opponents don't see where you have hidden your wolves.
2. When it's your turn, pick a point on your Opponent's Grid. *(Give an example, like C-3.)* If the other team has a wolf in that particular square on their Battlesheep Grid, you've found a wolf!
3. If you hit a wolf, mark the location on your Opponent's Grid with an "X." Pick up a "Fear" card, read it, and answer the question. When you're done, it's your opponent's turn.
4. If you didn't find a wolf, mark the location with an "O," a miss. If you didn't hit a wolf, it is your opponent's turn. You do not pick up and read a Fear Card.
5. Take turns until all your opponent's wolves have been found, or until you run out of time.

MOVE from group to group, answering questions and listening to what the children are saying.

FEAR CARD QUESTIONS

1. You were separated from your mom at the grocery store. You are alone and scared. What promise can you remember? What do you do?
2. You wake up in the middle of the night because of a loud thunderstorm. The lights are out and you are scared. What can you pray for? What do you do?
3. You have to read a poem at the school program. You get nervous in front of a lot of people. What do you pray for? What do you do?
4. You are starting your first day in a new school. You are hoping that you will like your teacher and meet some new friends. What promise can you remember? What do you do?
5. You cracked a window in your house when you were playing ball with your brother. You have to go tell your mom the truth. What do you pray for? What do you do?
6. You are waiting to meet your new babysitter. You are hoping that you will have a good time together. What can you pray for? What do you do?
7. You didn't finish your homework to turn into your teacher. You are not sure what will happen to you. What can you pray for? What do you do?
8. You want to take your favorite teddy bear to a slumber party, but you are afraid your friends will laugh at you. What promise do you remember? What do you do?
9. You have to go to the doctor to get a shot. You hate getting shots, and you are nervous all the way to the doctor's office. What can you pray for? What do you do?

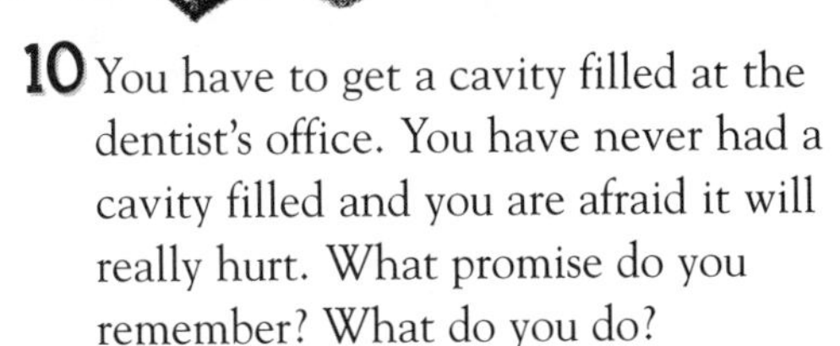

10 You have to get a cavity filled at the dentist's office. You have never had a cavity filled and you are afraid it will really hurt. What promise do you remember? What do you do?

11 You are standing on the edge of the diving board for the first time. It is very high, and you aren't sure you can dive off of it. All your friends are watching. What can you pray for? What do you do?

12 You are reading aloud in your class, and you aren't a very good reader. You are afraid everyone will laugh at you when you read. What do you remember about Jesus? What do you do?

13 You are in the lunch line at school and you just realized you don't have enough money to buy lunch. What can you pray for? What do you do?

14 You are staying over at a friend's house for the first time and you miss your mom. What promise can you remember? What do you do?

15 You are playing a new song at your first piano concert. You have practiced very hard, but you are still nervous. What do you pray for? What do you do?

16 You are playing ball with your brother in your yard. You run for a pass and trample your neighbor's favorite rose bush. Your parents say you have to tell them what happened. What do you pray for? What do you do?

WRAP-UP

SAY, "That was a fun game and a great way to help us learn how we can defeat our fears. When we pray and remember that Jesus is always with us, we can learn to trust the Good Shepherd to help us when we are afraid. **WE, LIKE SHEEP, ARE AFRAID AND NEED JESUS THE GOOD SHEPHERD TO COMFORT US.**"

BIBLE VERSE

GIVE a Bible Verse Card to each child and repeat the verse together. "I will fear no evil, for you are with me. Your rod and staff comfort me." Psalm 23:4

REMIND the kids, "This means that Jesus, the Good Shepherd, will protect us and keep us safe. If we follow what He tells us, we do not need to be afraid."

PRAYER

Dear God, Thank You for being our Good Shepherd. Thank You that You love us so much, You are with us all the time and will help us when we are afraid. This week, please help us to defeat our fears by praying, remembering Your promises, and remembering You are with us. Amen.

KID CONNECTION CONTINUES . . .

Small Group Leaders, use this time to continue to build community and learn more about your kids and their concerns. Listen closely so you are better equipped to pray for and reach out to each child.

ASK, "How could you help someone else who is afraid? Do you think you can learn to become less afraid? Why or why not?"

It's what JeSuS would do.
FoRGiVe A WoLF FoR FRee!
GRoWtH
I love ewe!
Hi

Unit 3: Show Me the Shepherd

The Good Shepherd Meets Needs

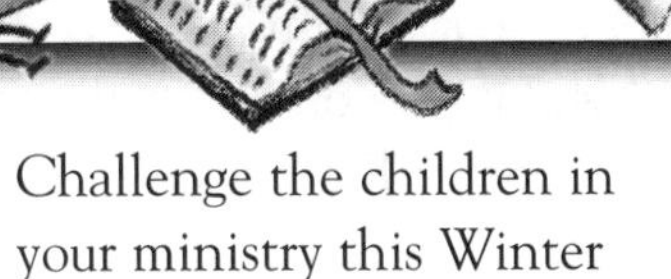

Challenge the children in your ministry this Winter Quarter as you present four of the 5-Gs: **Grace**, **Growth**, **Group**, and **Gift**. Unit 1 powerfully illustrates the **Group** and **Grace** "Gs" as Small Groups celebrate Christmas and kids hear about the "Unstoppable Love" God showed when He sent His Son, Jesus, to earth. In Unit 2, **Growth** and **Gift** are emphasized as kids learn from Jesus' example how to live "The Extreme Life." This quarter ends with Unit 3, "Show Me the Shepherd." Children will **Grow** as they explore how we are like sheep and Jesus is our Good Shepherd, and experience **Grace** when they hear the salvation message. Throughout the quarter, kids will learn more about what it means to "do life with God in the picture."

BIBLE SUMMARY

Psalm 23:1, 3; Proverbs 2:8; Matthew 6:25-33; Philippians 4:19

Children will learn that Jesus, the Good Shepherd, takes care of us. They will learn that He promises to protect those who follow Him. He forgives us when we sin. He promises to meet our needs. They will explore the difference between needs and wants and see how Jesus meets our needs.

KEY CONCEPT
Jesus, the Good Shepherd, knows our needs and can take care of us.

BIBLE VERSE

"The Lord is my shepherd. He gives me everything I need." Psalm 23:1 (*NIrV*)

OBJECTIVES

KNOW WHAT (LG): Children will hear how a shepherd meets the needs of his sheep and hear how Jesus meets our needs.

SO WHAT (LG): Children will learn that Jesus, our Good Shepherd, will give us what we need.

NOW WHAT (SG): Children will do an activity to discover the difference between needs and wants and thank God for meeting their needs.

SPIRITUAL FORMATION

Trust/Thanksgiving

5-G

Growth/Group

IN ADVANCE
(DONE BY YOUR ADMINISTRATOR)

- Photocopy and cut out Bible Verse Cards—one per child (page 59 in *Administrator's Guidebook*).
- Photocopy Desert Island Pictures—one for every pair of children (page 60 in *Administrator's Guidebook*).
- Gather pencils—one per every pair of children.
- Place the above-mentioned items in a bin for each Small Group Leader.

LEADER'S PREP

Read Psalm 23:1, 3; Proverbs 2:8; Matt. 6:25-33; Phil. 4:19. If a sheep eats too much or its wool is too heavy, it can fall, roll onto

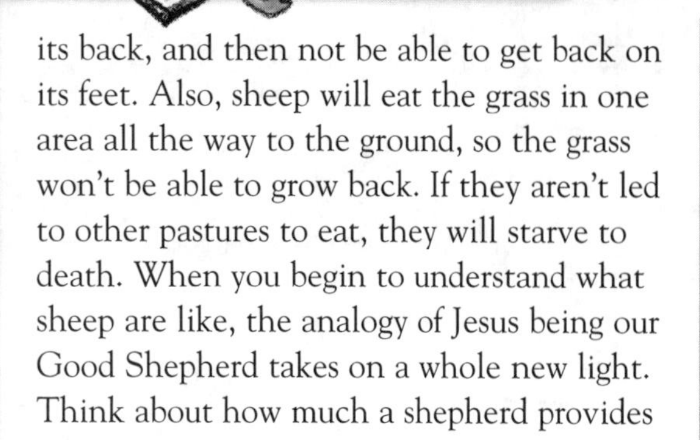

its back, and then not be able to get back on its feet. Also, sheep will eat the grass in one area all the way to the ground, so the grass won't be able to grow back. If they aren't led to other pastures to eat, they will starve to death. When you begin to understand what sheep are like, the analogy of Jesus being our Good Shepherd takes on a whole new light. Think about how much a shepherd provides for and protects his sheep. Jesus, our Good Shepherd, will provide for and protect us better than a shepherd provides for his sheep. You might read Matthew 6:25-33 every day this week. See if it helps to cultivate trust in Jesus' provision for you each day, and gratitude for all the ways that He meets your needs.

KID CONNECTION

(5 minutes)

WELCOME the kids to your Small Group.
ASK, "What is a toy or game you really want right now?"
SAY, "We all want things, but are they things we really need? Sometimes we get confused between what we want and what we need. I'm going to read our verse for today. It says, "The Lord is my shepherd. He gives me everything I need." Psalm 23:1 (*NIrV*) What do you think that verse means?" (*Jesus is our Shepherd, and He provides for us.*)

TRANSITION

SAY, "Today in Large Group, we are going to learn about how a shepherd cares for the needs of his sheep, and how Jesus, our Good Shepherd, cares for us. Listen to find out how a shepherd meets the needs of his sheep."

SMALL GROUP

(20 minutes)

REVIEW

ASK, "In what three ways does a shepherd meet the needs of His sheep? (*He protects, picks them up, and provides.*) What is the difference between needs and wants?" (*A need is something you must have in order to survive, and a want is something you'd like to have.*)
SAY, "**WE LEARNED THAT JESUS, THE GOOD SHEPHERD, KNOWS OUR NEEDS AND CAN TAKE CARE OF US.** Now, we're going to play a game where we can think more about things we need and things we want. To do this, we are going to work in pairs to see what we would need to survive on a deserted island."

ACTIVITY: DESERT ISLAND SURVIVAL

Our hope is that during Small Group Time, kids will begin to see the

SHEPHERDING TIP

With the barrage of "stuff" kids see on TV, they can easily become confused over what is a true need. Try to get them thinking outside our materialistic cutlure, and focus things a human being needs to actually survive.

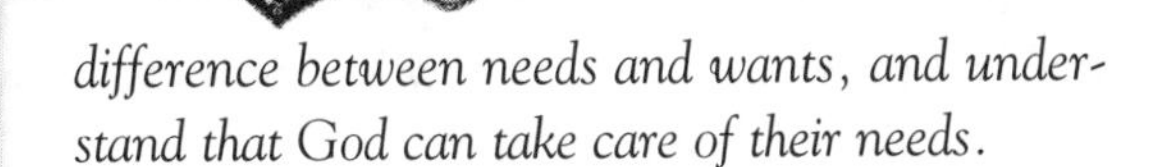

difference between needs and wants, and understand that God can take care of their needs.

SUPPLIES PROVIDED BY YOUR ADMINISTRATOR

- Desert Island Pictures
- Pencils

SET-UP

DIVIDE the kids in your group into pairs. Try to pair up kids who don't normally sit together.
GIVE each pair a Desert Island Picture.

INSTRUCTIONS

ASK, "Imagine you are stranded on this desert island. What would your needs be? (*Food, shelter, clothing, water*) What is one thing you might really want if you were stuck on an island, but you wouldn't need in order to survive?" (*Cookies, toys, TV*)
SAY, "Imagine you are stranded on a deserted island. You have nothing with you except what you are wearing. You can, however, use anything on or around the island to help you survive. Work with your partner to decide what you would use on the island to help you survive. Circle the things that you think you could use, and on the back of your picture, write their uses. For example, a bottle washed up on the shore could be used to hold drinking water. Go ahead and start."
ALLOW children time to work on the activity, leaving time to go over the answers. Spend a minute talking with each pair. Help with spelling, and encourage them to only write down a word or two to remind them of an item's use. Give kids a two-minute notice before the end of the activity.
GATHER the children together and have each pair explain their items and uses.
EXPLAIN, "You just circled things that you needed to help you survive on the deserted island. We talked earlier about what we wanted on the island. Your island probably didn't have everything you wanted, but you learned how to use what you were given to meet your needs. Jesus *can* provide all we need, but that doesn't mean He will always give us everything we want. Why do you suppose He might sometimes let us go without? *(To help us grow, to teach us lessons, to help us learn the difference between needs and wants)* Have you ever been in a situation where you thought Jesus wasn't going to meet your needs? (*I was really thirsty and didn't have any water, etc . . .*)

WRAP-UP

SAY, "Great job on that activity! We have a lot for which we can be thankful, even if we don't always get everything we want. **JESUS, THE GOOD SHEPHERD, KNOWS OUR NEEDS AND CAN TAKE CARE OF US**. We can trust Him that He will continue to meet our needs."

BIBLE VERSE

GIVE a Bible Verse Card to each child and repeat the verse together. "The Lord is my shepherd. He gives me everything I need." Psalm 23:1 (*NIrV*)
REMIND the kids, "This verse means that Jesus is our Good Shepherd, and we do not lack anything we need, because He is there to protect us, pick us up, and provide for us."

PRAYER

Dear God, thank You for Jesus, our Good Shepherd. Thank You for meeting all our needs. Please help us to follow You and trust You to take care of us. Amen.

KID CONNECTION CONTINUES . . .

Small Group Leaders, use this time to continue to build community and learn more about your kids and their concerns. Listen closely so you are better equipped to pray for and reach out to each child.

ASK, "Tell us about a time when you gave someone something they needed. How did that feel?"

Unit 3: Show Me the Shepherd

We, Like Sheep, Have Gone Astray

Challenge the children in your ministry this Winter Quarter as you present four of the 5-Gs: **Grace**, **Growth**, **Group**, and **Gift**. Unit 1 powerfully illustrates the **Group** and **Grace** "Gs" as Small Groups celebrate Christmas and kids hear about the "Unstoppable Love" God showed when He sent His Son, Jesus, to earth. In Unit 2, **Growth** and **Gift** are emphasized as kids learn from Jesus' example how to live "The Extreme Life." This quarter ends with Unit 3, "Show Me the Shepherd." Children will **Grow** as they explore how we are like sheep and Jesus is our Good Shepherd, and experience **Grace** when they hear the salvation message. Throughout the quarter, kids will learn more about what it means to "do life with God in the picture."

BIBLE SUMMARY

Isaiah 53:6, Psalm 23:6, Matthew 6:19, Philippians 4:8

In this lesson, the children will learn how sheep tend to wander off, just like we tend to wander away from Jesus. They will learn how a Good Shepherd sets limits to protect the sheep, and see how Jesus sets limits to protect us from harm. They will learn that they will be safe and live the best life if they stay within Jesus' limits.

KEY CONCEPT
We, like sheep, go astray so Jesus, the Good Shepherd, sets limits.

BIBLE VERSE

"All we like sheep have gone astray." Isaiah 53:6

OBJECTIVES

KNOW WHAT: (LG) Children will hear how sheep tend to wander off and how a shepherd sets limits. The result of staying within the limits is that we will be safe.
SO WHAT: (LG) Children will learn that Jesus, our Good Shepherd, has set limits in the Bible to keep us from going astray.
NOW WHAT: (SG) Children will do an activity to explore the benefits of staying within the limits Jesus has set in the Bible.

SPIRITUAL FORMATION

Study Scriptures/Obedience

5-G

Growth/Group

IN ADVANCE
(DONE BY YOUR ADMINISTRATOR)

- Photocopy and cut out Bible Verse Cards—one per child (page 65 in *Administrator's Guidebook*).
- Photocopy and cut out Direction Cards—one set per group (pages 61-64 in *Administrator's Guidebook*).
- Photocopy Sheep Pen Gameboard—one per group (pages 66-67 in *Administrator's Guidebook*). Take the pages out of the book and line up the inner seams to make

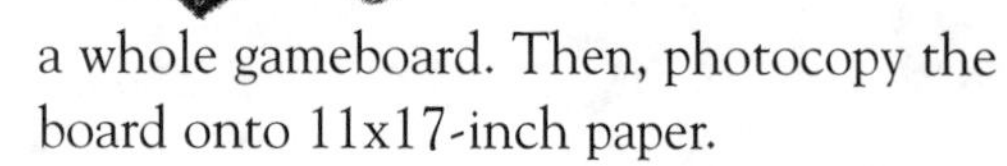

a whole gameboard. Then, photocopy the board onto 11x17-inch paper.

- Gather Game Pieces—ten per group, five of one color and five of another color. You can use erasers, candies, game pieces from a board game, or squares of cardstock.
- Place the above-mentioned items in a bin for each Small Group Leader.

LEADER'S PREP

Read Isaiah 53:6, Psalm 23:6, Philippians 4:8, Matthew 6:19. Over the past few weeks, we've learned that sheep really can't survive on their own. A shepherd must protect and care for the sheep. When sheep stay within the shepherd's care, they are safe, happy and healthy. When they stray, who knows what will happen to them? Maybe a wolf will attack or the sheep will wander into a dangerous place. We are like sheep, too, prone to stray and wander from the care of the Good Shepherd. In the Bible, Jesus lays out the limits for us. We need to live within these limits in order to live a safe life. Take some time this week to thank God for the limits He gives us and recognize that those limits are motivated by His incredible love and knowledge of what is best for us. Think about areas in your life where you tend to stray, and make plans to live within the safety of the Good Shepherd's loving care.

KID CONNECTION

(5 minutes)

WELCOME the kids to Promiseland.
ASK, "What rules do you have at school or home? What happens if you follow the rules? Why might you want to break a rule? What might happen if you break a rule?"
SAY, "Breaking the rules can have bad consequences. When we follow the rules, we are protected and safe."

TRANSITION

TELL the kids, "Last week, we learned that a good shepherd cares for the needs of his sheep. Then, we learned that Jesus, our Good Shepherd, can take care of our needs. Today in Large Group, we are going to learn more about sheep, and how we are like sheep. Listen to find out why a shepherd puts limits on the sheep."

SMALL GROUP

(20 minutes)

REVIEW

ASK, "Why does a shepherd set limits or boundaries for the sheep? *(To protect them and keep them safe.)* Where can we learn about the limits Jesus has set for us?" *(The Bible)*

SAY, "WE LEARNED THAT WE, LIKE SHEEP, GO ASTRAY, SO THE GOOD SHEPHERD SETS LIMITS. We really need Jesus, the Good Shepherd, to put up fences, or limits, to help keep us safe. Today we are going to play a game to help us think

SHEPHERDING TIP
When discussing the situations, make sure to allow for discussion about positive consequences of staying within the limits and negative consequences of straying from those limits.

about the benefits of staying within the limits Jesus has set for us in the Bible."

ACTIVITY: PROTECT YOUR SHEEP

The purpose of this activity is to help kids think about Jesus' limits in a positive way.

SUPPLIES PROVIDED BY YOUR ADMINISTRATOR

- ❍ Sheep Pen Gameboard
- ❍ Direction Cards
- ❍ Game Pieces

SET-UP

DIVIDE the group into two teams.
LAY the Sheep Pen Gameboard in the middle of your group.
PUT five Game Pieces for each team in the Sheep Herd spots.
LAY Direction Cards face down next to the gameboard.

INSTRUCTIONS

SAY, "Your Game Pieces represent sheep. The object of this game is to move all your sheep safely on the path from the pasture to the sheep pen. The team that gets all their sheep safely to the pen first is the winner."
SAY, "When it is your team's turn, you will pick a Direction Card. Answer it and move your sheep along the path to the farm. Then, it is the other team's turn. Within your teams, you will take turns reading the card and moving the "sheep" game piece. As a team, you will have five sheep to move along the path. The first team to get all five sheep safely to the pen will be the winner. You will move one sheep all the way into the pen before starting another one."
SAY, "Follow the directions on the card you draw. The first team with all of their sheep in the pen is the winner."
CHOOSE one team to go first.
CONTINUE playing until one team moves all their sheep to the pen.

DIRECTION CARD EXAMPLES

- Your sheep wanders from the shepherd. Lose a turn.
- Your sheep falls down. Go back 1 space.
- Your sheep follows the crowd. Go back 2 spaces.
- A wolf comes and tries to attack the sheep. Go back to start.
- "Do not lie to each other." Colossians 3:9 Your mom asks you if you cleaned your room. You didn't clean it yet. You have the opportunity to lie or to tell the truth. What are the benefits of telling the truth? What are the consequences of lying? (Move forward 3 spaces)
- "Do not let any unwholesome talk come out of your mouths, but only what is helpful for building others up according to their needs." Ephesians 4:29 You are with your friends, and they are talking about the new kid in your class. You can say something nice about him/her or you can say something mean. What are the benefits of saying something nice? What are the consequences of saying something mean? (Move forward 2 spaces)
- "Children, obey your parents in the Lord, for this is right." Ephesians 6:1 You are home alone after school. Your mom tells you not to use the oven. You are hungry and want a snack. You could use the oven or eat some

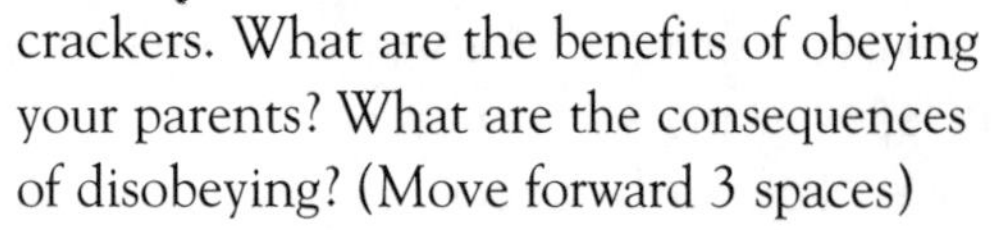

crackers. What are the benefits of obeying your parents? What are the consequences of disobeying? (Move forward 3 spaces)

- True or False? Sheep are very dumb. (True. Move 2 spaces)
- True or False? Sheep can fall down and not be able to get up. (True. Move 3 spaces)
- True or False? Sheep are calm animals and don't become scared easily. (False. Move 2 spaces)
- What happens if one sheep becomes scared and starts to run? (All the other sheep follow. Move 3 spaces)
- True or False? The Bible tells us that we are like sheep. (True. Move 2 spaces)
- Who is the Good Shepherd? (Jesus. Move 3 spaces)
- True or False? Sheep need to have a good shepherd to take care of them. (True. Move 2 spaces)
- True or False? Sheep will eat the grass in one area down to the soil and not know to look for more food elsewhere. (True. Move 3 spaces)
- True or False? Shepherds don't have to provide for the sheep. (False. Move 2 spaces)
- Name one way we are like sheep. (We follow the crowd. We are clueless to danger. We need a shepherd, etc. Move 4 spaces)
- True or False? Sheep can wander in a pasture freely with no shepherd watching over them and be safe. (False. Move 3 spaces)
- True or False? Sheep follow each other. (True. Move 2 spaces)
- What is the difference between a need and a want? (A need is something you have to have to live. A want is something you'd like to have. Move 3 spaces)
- True or False? Sheep can be irritated by bugs that nest in their wool. (True. Move 2 spaces)
- True or False? Sheep need to stay in the protection of the shepherd. (True. Move 3 spaces)
- Move right to the pen!

WRAP UP

SAY, "Good job moving your sheep into the pen! **WE, LIKE SHEEP, GO ASTRAY SO THE GOOD SHEPHERD SETS LIMITS** for us, just like a shepherd builds a fence for his sheep. We don't always follow the shepherd. But, when we stay within the limits Jesus sets for us in the Bible, we can live the best life and the Good Shepherd can keep us safe."

BIBLE VERSE

GIVE a Bible Verse Card to each child and repeat the verse together. "All we like sheep have gone astray." Isaiah 53:6

REMIND the kids, "This verse means that we wander away from the limits God sets for us in the Bible. But, we can read the Bible and learn how to stay within His limits."

PRAYER

Dear God, thank You for loving us so much that you set limits to keep us safe. Thank You for giving us the Bible so we can read and understand those limits. This week, help us to live within the limits You have set for us. Amen.

KID CONNECTION CONTINUES . . .

Small Group Leaders, use this time to continue to build community and learn more about your kids and their concerns. Listen closely so you are better equipped to pray for and reach out to each child.

ASK, "Why do you think your parents set certain limits and have certain rules for you?"

Don't call us... we'll call ewe!
SHEPHERDS WANTED

Unit 3: Show Me the Shepherd

The Good Shepherd Laid Down His Life for the Sheep

Challenge the children in your ministry this Winter Quarter as you present four of the 5-Gs: **Grace**, **Growth**, **Group**, and **Gift**. Unit 1 powerfully illustrates the **Group** and **Grace** "Gs" as Small Groups celebrate Christmas and kids hear about the "Unstoppable Love" God showed when He sent His Son, Jesus, to earth. In Unit 2, **Growth** and **Gift** are emphasized as kids learn from Jesus' example how to live "The Extreme Life." This quarter ends with Unit 3, "Show Me the Shepherd." Children will **Grow** as they explore how we are like sheep and Jesus is our Good Shepherd, and experience **Grace** when they hear the salvation message. Throughout the quarter, kids will learn more about what it means to "do life with God in the picture."

KEY CONCEPT
Jesus, the Good Shepherd, laid down His life for us, His sheep.

BIBLE SUMMARY

Isaiah 53:6; John 3:16; 10:11-16, 25-28

In this lesson, the children will continue to learn how we are like sheep. They will learn about dangers sheep face and that a good shepherd will lay down his life for the sheep. They will learn that Jesus, the Good Shepherd, laid down His life for us by dying on the cross for our sins. They will have the opportunity to respond to the salvation message.

BIBLE VERSE

"The Good Shepherd lays down His life for the sheep." John 10:1

OBJECTIVES

KNOW WHAT: (LG) Children will hear that Jesus is the Good Shepherd who laid down His life for us, His sheep.
SO WHAT: (LG) Children will learn that Jesus died to take the punishment for our sins and give us eternal life.
NOW WHAT: (SG) Children will hear stories from Small Group Leaders who have admitted they have gone astray (sinned), believed that Jesus, the Good Shepherd, took the punishment for their sin, and have chosen to follow Him.

SPIRITUAL FORMATION

Salvation

5-G

Grace/Group

IN ADVANCE
(DONE BY YOUR ADMINISTRATOR)

- Photocopy and cut out Bible Verse Cards—one per child (page 68 in *Administrator's Guidebook*).
- Photocopy Show Me the Shepherd Booklets—one per child (pages 69-70 in *Administrator's Guidebook*). Cut out the booklets, assemble them, and staple the spines.

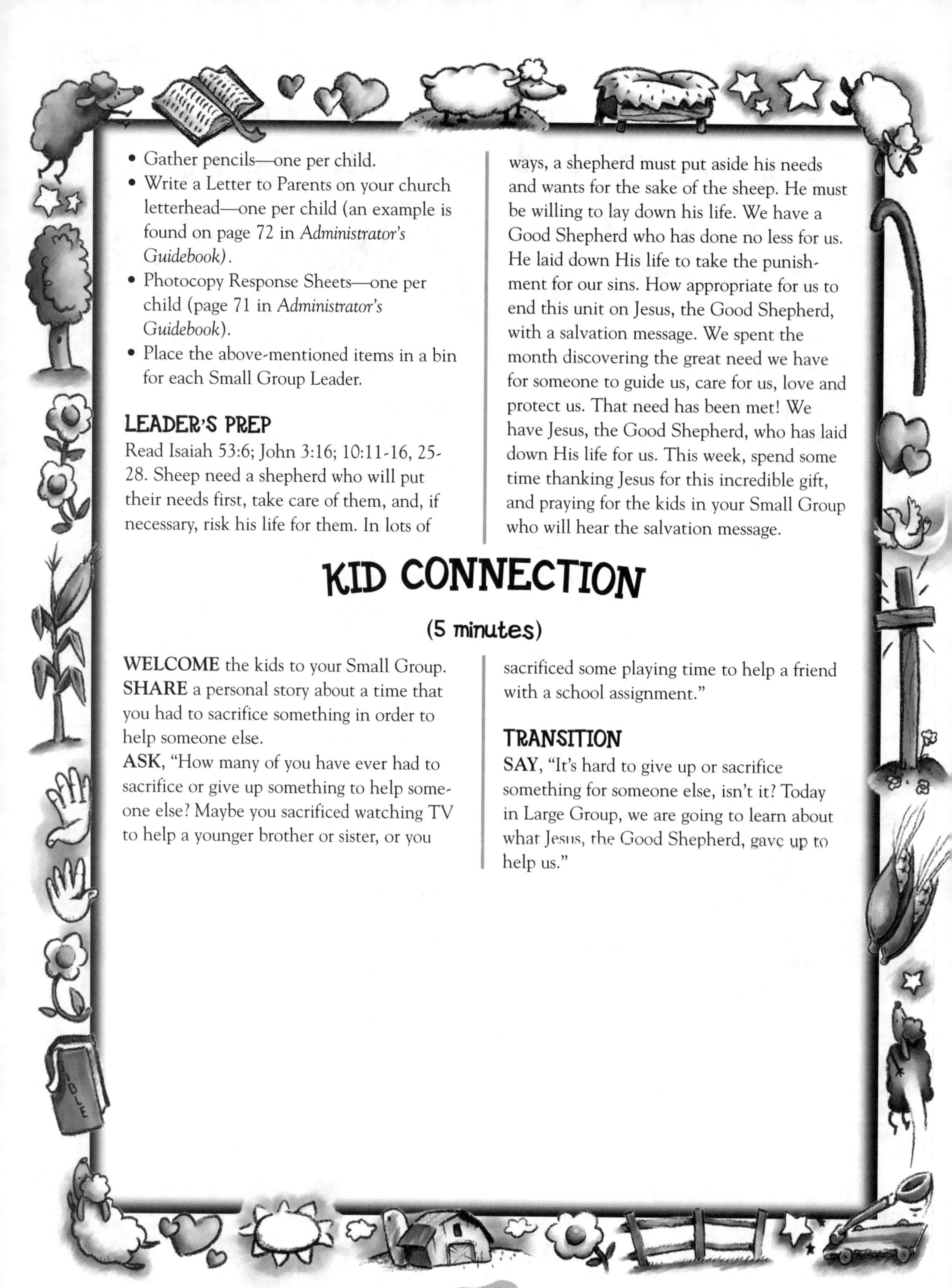

- Gather pencils—one per child.
- Write a Letter to Parents on your church letterhead—one per child (an example is found on page 72 in *Administrator's Guidebook)*.
- Photocopy Response Sheets—one per child (page 71 in *Administrator's Guidebook*).
- Place the above-mentioned items in a bin for each Small Group Leader.

LEADER'S PREP

Read Isaiah 53:6; John 3:16; 10:11-16, 25-28. Sheep need a shepherd who will put their needs first, take care of them, and, if necessary, risk his life for them. In lots of ways, a shepherd must put aside his needs and wants for the sake of the sheep. He must be willing to lay down his life. We have a Good Shepherd who has done no less for us. He laid down His life to take the punishment for our sins. How appropriate for us to end this unit on Jesus, the Good Shepherd, with a salvation message. We spent the month discovering the great need we have for someone to guide us, care for us, love and protect us. That need has been met! We have Jesus, the Good Shepherd, who has laid down His life for us. This week, spend some time thanking Jesus for this incredible gift, and praying for the kids in your Small Group who will hear the salvation message.

KID CONNECTION

(5 minutes)

WELCOME the kids to your Small Group.
SHARE a personal story about a time that you had to sacrifice something in order to help someone else.
ASK, "How many of you have ever had to sacrifice or give up something to help someone else? Maybe you sacrificed watching TV to help a younger brother or sister, or you sacrificed some playing time to help a friend with a school assignment."

TRANSITION

SAY, "It's hard to give up or sacrifice something for someone else, isn't it? Today in Large Group, we are going to learn about what Jesus, the Good Shepherd, gave up to help us."

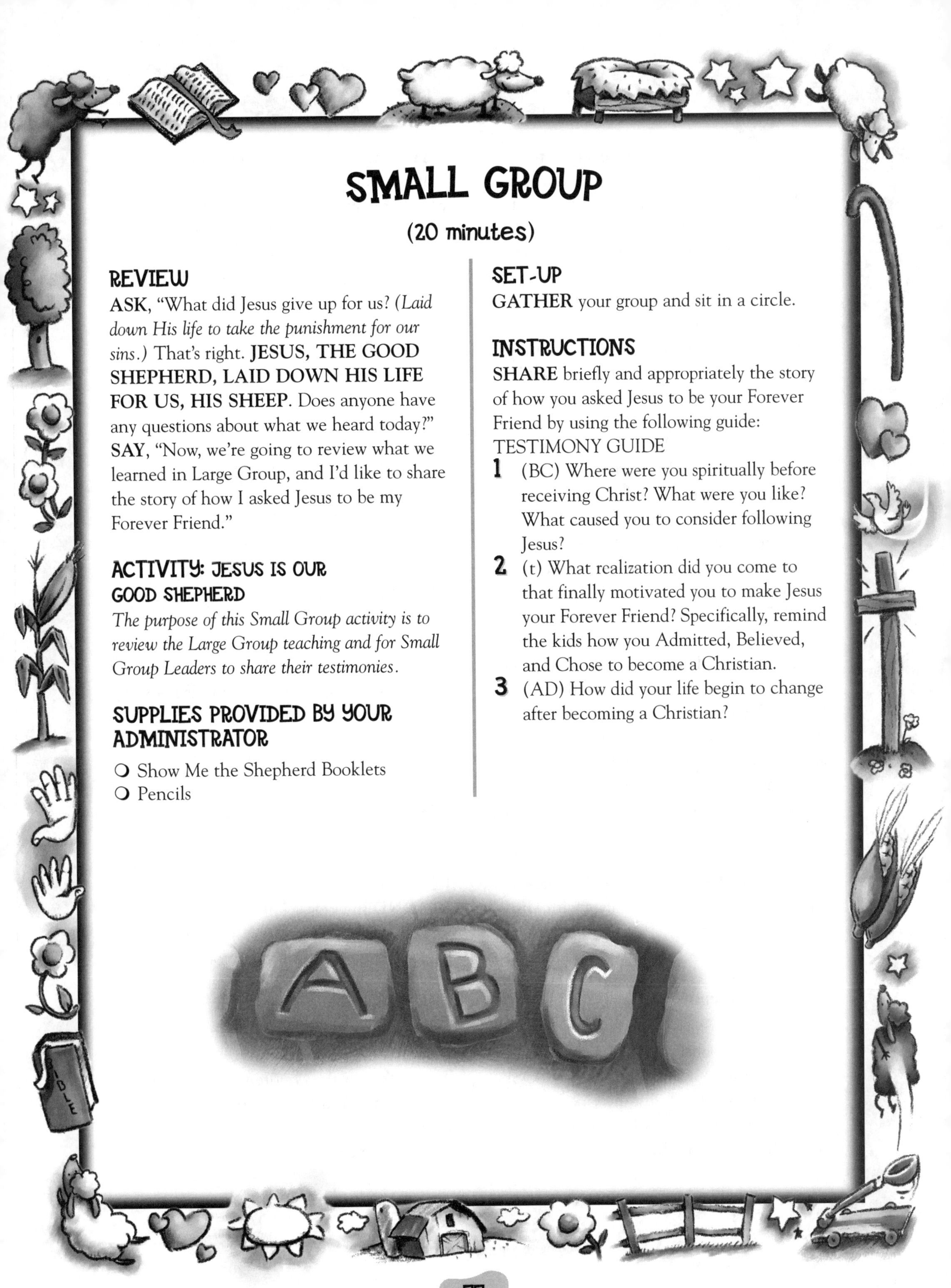

SMALL GROUP

(20 minutes)

REVIEW

ASK, "What did Jesus give up for us? *(Laid down His life to take the punishment for our sins.)* That's right. **JESUS, THE GOOD SHEPHERD, LAID DOWN HIS LIFE FOR US, HIS SHEEP**. Does anyone have any questions about what we heard today?" **SAY**, "Now, we're going to review what we learned in Large Group, and I'd like to share the story of how I asked Jesus to be my Forever Friend."

ACTIVITY: JESUS IS OUR GOOD SHEPHERD

The purpose of this Small Group activity is to review the Large Group teaching and for Small Group Leaders to share their testimonies.

SUPPLIES PROVIDED BY YOUR ADMINISTRATOR

- ❍ Show Me the Shepherd Booklets
- ❍ Pencils

SET-UP

GATHER your group and sit in a circle.

INSTRUCTIONS

SHARE briefly and appropriately the story of how you asked Jesus to be your Forever Friend by using the following guide:
TESTIMONY GUIDE

1. (BC) Where were you spiritually before receiving Christ? What were you like? What caused you to consider following Jesus?
2. (t) What realization did you come to that finally motivated you to make Jesus your Forever Friend? Specifically, remind the kids how you Admitted, Believed, and Chose to become a Christian.
3. (AD) How did your life begin to change after becoming a Christian?

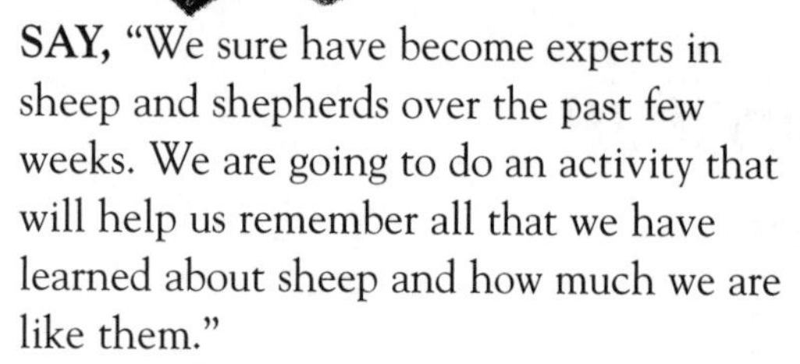

SAY, "We sure have become experts in sheep and shepherds over the past few weeks. We are going to do an activity that will help us remember all that we have learned about sheep and how much we are like them."

GIVE a Show Me the Shepherd Booklet and pencil to each child.

SAY, "Open your booklet to page 2. This picture shows our problem. We can't get to heaven to be with God. Draw a sheep on the left-hand side of the page. Can anyone remember what it is that separates us from God and the sheepfold? *(sin)* That's right, sin. Write the word sin, S-I-N, in the space between the sheep and the sheepfold. Fortunately, we have a Good Shepherd who loves us very much and does not want to be separated from us."

SAY, "Turn to page 4. Again, draw a sheep on the left-hand side of the page. Jesus, the Good Shepherd, helps us with this sin problem. Who remembers what Jesus, the Good Shepherd, did for us? *(He laid down His own life on the cross to take the punishment for our sins.)* Draw a cross between the sheep and the sheep fold. Now what happens to us? *(We can be Forever Friends with God.)* Finally, draw a sheep safely in the sheep fold. The Good Shepherd loves us and cares so much, He laid down His life so we can be Forever Friends with Him, and live safely with Him in heaven forever."

SAY, "Turn to page 6 to see what we need to do to start a Forever Friendship with God. 'A' is for ADMIT. We admit we have sinned and we ask for forgiveness. 'B' is for BELIEVE. We believe that Jesus took the punishment for our sins. 'C' is for CHOOSE. We choose to follow Jesus, the Good Shepherd, and be Forever Friends with Him. Write those words in the blanks provided."

SAY, "On page 7, write your name in the blank if you know you need Jesus, the Good Shepherd, and you have or want to have a Forever Friendship with Jesus. If you became Forever Friends with Jesus for the first time today, write the date on the line below your name."

WRAP UP

GIVE Response Sheets to the children.

HAVE kids fill in their names and addresses.

ASK kids to listen carefully as you read the three statements on the sheet.

HAVE the kids mark the appropriate boxes on the Response Sheets, then fill in the other information on the sheet.

COLLECT the Response Sheets.

GIVE a Parent Letter to each child.

EXPLAIN to the kids, "If you asked Jesus to be your Forever Friend today, or if you have done so in the past, you are now in God's family forever. If you did not pray today, God still loves you and wants to be your Forever Friend. You can take this step whenever you are ready."

BIBLE VERSE

GIVE a Bible Verse Card to each child and repeat the verse together. "The Good Shepherd lays down His life for the sheep." John 10:11

REMIND the kids, "This verse means that Jesus laid down His life to save us, so that we can live with Him in heaven forever."

PRAYER

Dear God, Thank You for sending Your Son, Jesus, to take the punishment for our sin. Thank You for the children here today who just accepted You as their Forever Friend. Please be with those who are still thinking about it. Amen.

KID CONNECTION CONTINUES . . .

RETURN to Large Group for a music celebration.
TALLY the responses from the Response Sheets onto one blank Response Sheet.

GIVE that tallied Response Sheet to your Administrator. Save your kids' sheets for yourself.

FORGIVE A WOLF FOR FREE!
GOD'S SHEEP FOLD
SHEPHERDS WANTED
Don't call us... we'll call ewe!
Gifts
GOOD STEWARDSHIP
GRACE
A B C
Hee Hee!
SHEARING FOR SHARING